INTERNATIONAL POCKET LIBRARY
EDITED BY EDMUND R. BROWN

TWO TALES BY RUDYARD KIPLING

TWO TALES BY RUDYARD KIPLING

THE MAN WHO WOULD BE KING

—

WITHOUT BENEFIT OF CLERGY

INTRODUCTION BY WILSON FOLLETT

BOSTON
INTERNATIONAL POCKET LIBRARY

First printing, 5,000 copies
Second printing, 5,000 copies
Third printing, 5,000 copies
Fourth printing, 10,000 copies

Fifth printing, 5,000 copies

1984

Branden Publishing Company Inc.
21 Station Street Box 843
Brookline Village MA 02147

INTRODUCTION

I

THERE are two contradictory views of Mr. Rudyard Kipling, both of them made familiar by much repetition, and both vital enough so that in twenty years neither has given any special promise of eventually supplanting the other. The first view is that Mr. Kipling is an accomplished and industrious journalist turned man of letters, gathering and reporting novelties with all the journalist's facility; subject to most of the journalistic limitations, and subject also, finally and above all, to the limitations of an old-fashioned imperialistic and rather brutal philosophy which, for the twentieth century and men growing toward a humane and idealistic internationalism, is simply not good enough. The other view is that Mr. Kipling is all objective artist, obsessed by no other concern than the artist's own authentic concern for beauty—the beauty of the successive forms and images into which he translates for us so much of life as he has seen, heard, imagined, felt. The one interpretation makes Kipling a sort of propagandist—first, of "the white man's burden," of imperial rule in general as against that principle which we have lately learned to call "the self-determination of peoples"; secondly and specifically, of British imperialism against all other. The second interpretation insists that, however much he may have written *about* British imperialism, it is no real part of his function to write *for* it; that, if the artist be sensitive enough to life, it makes no conceivable difference what special aspects of life happen to have come under his notice; that, in fine, all of Mr. Kipling's poems and tales of Anglo-Indian life present, not arguments, but aspects—aspects chosen from a body of fact which, being at once real, picturesque, and momentous, will serve as well as another.

Mr. John Palmer has interestingly expressed* this second possible view of Kipling, in connection with an attempt to prove that Kipling's grim levity, his brutality, his cynicism, his sometimes irritating flippancy, his *sécheresse du cœur*, are all deliberately invoked for æsthetic ends—as guards against sentimentality, and as guides to that truth whose very ruthlessness is beauty. The qualities of hardness which have sometimes been traced to the imperialistic strain in Kipling the man, Mr. Palmer traces to the sensitiveness of Kipling the artist, the instant responsiveness of his temperament to the demands of his subjects to be handled in a particular way.

It is nothing to the present purpose to deny that there is a deal of truth in the first of these two estimates; but it may very well be questioned whether it puts the accent in the right place. Both accounts are true, or something more than half-true; but they are accounts of quite different phenomena. The first has to do with Mr. Kipling as a person and as a political thinker, and with the inferences about him which one might draw from the whole trend and sum of his work considered as personal revelation. The second is an account simply of the single-minded devotion

*In "Rudyard Kipling" (Writers of the Day). New York: Henry Holt and Company. This volume also contains a useful bibliography of the writings of Mr. Kipling.

with which, in this story and that taken by itself, an artist's imagination clothes in comeliness the abiding impression of an old memory or a new dream. If we were dealing in biography, these two would have a connection: we should read the man as self-betrayed in his work, the work as self-implied in the man. But when we are dealing in literature, in beautiful letters, and reading the works themselves for themselves, the two have no more intelligible connection than the worth of a jewel has with the casket which contains it. The attempt of the schools to make literature a clue to the man who wrote it, to the age in which it was produced, to various codes and notions of what ought to be done or not done,—to anything and everything other than the supreme power of the beautiful thing itself to make the moment eternal or "tease us out of thought,"—this attempt is the mortal enemy of literature, and almost the destruction of our sense of what literature is for. But we common readers know in our hearts that no man ever yet wrote, or could write, a supreme story in order to exalt the opinions and prejudices either of himself or of an age; and it is precisely by virtue of their freedom from these opinions and prejudices that the products of taste become of worth, and can survive the moment. In the instant of divination when we thrill to some luminous story for what it is in itself, forgetful quite of all the doubts and conjectures not raised by the story, then we understand what is the purport and the justification of letters. And if it be a tale from *Under the Deodars* or *Life's Handicap* or *Traffics and Discoveries*, we understand too that our debt is to that Kipling (by queer incidental mischance an imperialist and Anglophile fanatic) who has lived in order

to write stories—and not the least in the world to that
other Kipling, the professional patriot and exhorter to
material prestige, whom some allege merely to have drama-
tized his personal convictions in a handful of tales.

The story is, after all, the thing: for all the purposes of
literature, it makes no difference when or why it was written, or who wrote it, or what else he may also have written. When we read the best tales of Kipling, we are ex-
periencing parts which are genuinely greater and completer
than the whole; for those parts reach a consistency, a
symmetry, an inherent logic of beauty, quite lacking to the
whole personality and career which produced them. In
Kipling, taken as a whole, there is no such intellectual and
spiritual continuity as we find in, for example, Mr. Joseph
Conrad; no such disinterestedness of contemplation, no
such inexorable growth, no such cosmic sense of truth. But
in *The Drums of the Fore-and-Aft, Wireless,* "They," *The
Ship That Found Herself, The Man Who Was, The Man
Who Would Be King, Brugglesmith, Steam Tactics, The
Incarnation of Krishna Mulvaney*—in such stories as these
(not to prolong the list) you find little record of the ugly
limitations which belong to Kipling the citizen, Kipling
the representative of a certain cult of blood and iron and
efficiency, Kipling the junker. You find only a series of
consummate embodiments of some kinds of beauty—the
grim, the fantastic, the droll, the heroic, the pathetic.
There is just enough artist in Kipling to fill one small
shapely vessel at a time, and fill it full. Why, with these
glorious tales in our hands, should we not cherish them for
what they are, and leave the ignoble rest to homilists and
pundits?

II

The adaptability and virtuosity of the artist in Kipling could be illustrated within the scope of the present volume—a volume which seems to me precious out of all proportion to its size—in either of two ways.

The first way would be to select two tales of different periods as well as of different modes. Between, for example, *Without Benefit of Clergy* and *An Habitation Enforced* (in *Actions and Reactions*) the better sort of reader would trace a paradoxical kinship, a similarity in difference. *Without Benefit* is the tragic idyll of a love predestined to material failure and dissolution, a love snatched by puny human creatures in defiance of the strong will of the gods. Because Holden dares love Ameera across the barrier of race, the whole episode from beginning to end, for the lovers and for us, is saturated with the obscure sense of mortality. This sense of mortality is the ultimate perfection of the tragic in art. That the beauty which, in our forlorn lives, is most fragile and evanescent should become the very stuff of the eternal loveliness in art—that is the paradox of all greatest art, as fulfillment through abnegation is of all religions. Life gives the artist a series of broken arcs: he makes them into the perfect round, as he alone can do. Art can exist for life's sake only because life has first existed, all tragically incomplete as it is, for art's sake. *Without Benefit of Clergy* is the coherence and completion of art wrought out of the illogicality and dissolution of life. *An Habitation Enforced* is in some sort the converse of the earlier tale: it reverses the current of irony, it is a story of racial kinship deeply implanted, subtly at work against sundering circumstance, to bring back "after certain days," across an ocean and a gulf of generations, two children of the New World who have heard in their blood the call of the Old. Its theme—the theme, roughly, of *The Passionate Pilgrim* of Henry James—exists in the region of pure high comedy, whose function it is to present life in those rare fulfillments which occur when life's constant threat of disintegration is miraculously not carried out. *Without Benefit of Clergy* ends in the obliteration of the very scene: a surge of new life, of civilization, of progress, washes over the spot, " 'so that no man may say where this house stood.' " *An Habitation Enforced* ends in the renewing of an old structure for the sake of the time to come, in answer to the inexorable claims of generations yet unborn: " 'Make it oak then; we can't get out of it.' "

The unity-in-duality of such a selection would have the further merit of calling attention to the artistic validity of Kipling in some of his later, less popular manifestations. Criticism has been oddly cold to the volumes which follow the early Anglo-Indian period of Kipling; and it is to be suspected that popular applause has for once belied its traditional independence of professional applause. It is doing a small service to the honorable trade of criticism, as well as, by happy chance, a great service to some receptive reader here and there, to suggest that the Kipling most notable for adequacy is he of two later volumes, *Traffics and Discoveries* and *Actions and Reactions*.

There is, nevertheless, something to be said for the second and more conventional principle of selection here resorted to. The range of Kipling's effects would lose force in the very process of being illustrated by the work of dif-

ferent decades; for the mere lapse of time might account
for that variety which, I wish here to show, has belonged to
Kipling from the outset. In *Without Benefit of Clergy*
and *The Man Who Would Be King* we have, then, his
early period quintessentialized; and in the quite separate
and contrasted identities of these two tales, both exotic, we
have the measure of his variety—the more strikingly because it reveals the widest difference just where we might
count on the narrowest resemblance. We replace the con-
trast between tragic idyll and comic, from different periods,
with that between tragic idyll and tragic farce from the
same period. And of the two gaps the second seems, on
the whole, the wider.

The tale which is tragic farce, *The Man Who Would Be
King,* stands with one exception unapproached in English
among stories of the corrosion of human nature by the too
intimate contact of exploiting race with exploited. That
single exception, Mr. Joseph Conrad's *Heart of Darkness,*
is so vastly more cosmic in its humor, and is planned on so
vast and leisurely a scale, that it hardly allows itself to be
compared with the earlier tale in fairness to both. *The
Man Who Would Be King* may still be said, then, to remain incomparable in its own kind. Its sort of perfection
may indeed be trivial beside that of *Heart of Darkness*:
but then, it ought to be added that *The Man Who Would
Be King* renders trivial in turn Mr. Conrad's own earlier
treatment of the same theme in *An Outpost of Progress*—a
fairer object of comparison, because of approximately the
same dimensions as Kipling's tale. After all, *The Man
Who Would Be King* is perfect—and what profit is to be
got from the invidious comparison of perfections? The

mad Irishman Carnehan—a being so truly known and drawn that one hardly knows whether to call him more mad when he is mad than when he is sane—is all adequacy and utter truth from our first glimpse of him in the train at Nasirabad to the instant when his shriveled and ghastly head, still wearing the crown of gold, is jerked from the haircloth sack by the palsied hand of Dravot. This adequacy is the thing that finally matters. The tale is not some other tale by some other hand,—the fallacy of comparison being the half-suggestion that it ought to be,—but it is perfectly, consummately, exhaustively itself, and as unlike anything else of its own author as it is unlike anything at all of any other author.

If there remain a person to suggest that these stories, and the best of the others, must be second-rate and ephemeral because the author of them has sometimes been a brazen-throated prophet of expediency, and sometimes a patriot intolerant and insular, one can only suggest again to that person that he will never comprehend an artist by looking at him through political spectacles. We have to do here, not with any code or precept or programme, any formula or theory, any plea for or against imperialism or anything else; but only with two consummate narratives that will still exist and be beautiful, as now, in their strangely different ways, when all the local colorists have ceased from coloring, and the wicked realists are at rest.

WILSON FOLLETT

THE MAN WHO WOULD BE KING

THE MAN WHO WOULD BE KING

"Brother to a Prince and fellow to a beggar if he be found worthy."

THE LAW, as quoted, lays down a fair conduct of life, and one not easy to follow. I have been fellow to a beggar again and again under circumstances which prevented either of us finding out whether the other was worthy. I have still to be brother to a Prince, though I once came near to kinship with what might have been a veritable King and was promised the reversion of a Kingdom—army, law-courts, revenue and policy all complete. But, to-day, I greatly fear that my King is dead, and if I want a crown I must go and hunt for it myself.

The beginning of everything was in a railway train upon the road to Mhow from Ajmir. There had been a Deficit in the Budget, which necessitated traveling, not Second-class, which is only half as dear as First-class, but by Intermediate, which is very awful indeed. There are no cushions in the Intermediate class, and the population are either Intermediate, which is Eurasian, or native, which for a long night journey is nasty, or Loafer, which is amusing though intoxicated. Intermediates do not patronize refreshment-rooms. They carry their food in bundles and pots, and buy sweets from the native sweetmeat-sellers, and drink the roadside water. That is why in the hot weather Intermediates are taken out of the carriages dead, and in all weathers are most properly looked down upon.

My particular Intermediate happened to be empty till I reached Nasirabad, when a huge gentleman in shirt-sleeves entered, and, following the custom of Intermediates, passed the time of day. He was a wanderer and a vagabond like myself, but with an educated taste for whiskey. He told tales of things he had seen and done, of out-of-the-way corners of the Empire into which he had penetrated, and of adventures in which he risked his life for a few days' food. "If India was filled with men like you and me, not knowing more than the crows where they'd get their next days' rations, it isn't seventy millions of revenue the land would be paying—it's seven hundred millions," said he; and as I looked at his mouth and chin I was disposed to agree with him. We talked politics—the politics of Loaferdom that sees things from the underside where the lath and plaster is not smoothed off—and we talked postal arrangements because my friend wanted to send a telegram back from the next station to Ajmir, which is the turning-off place from the Bombay to the Mhow line as you travel westward. My friend had no money beyond eight annas which he wanted for dinner, and I had no money at all, owing to the hitch in the Budget before mentioned. Further, I was going into a wilderness where, though I should resume touch with the Treasury, there were no telegraph offices. I was, therefore, unable to help him in any way. "We might threaten a Station-master, and make him send a wire on tick," said my friend, "but that'd mean inquiries for you and for me, and I've got my hands full these days. Did you say you are traveling back along this line within any days?"

"Within ten," I said.

"Can't you make it eight?" said he. "Mine is rather urgent business."

"I can send your telegram within ten days if that will serve you," I said.

"I couldn't trust the wire to fetch him now I think of it. It's this way. He leaves Delhi on the 23d for Bombay. That means he'll be running through Ajmir about the night of the 23d."

"But I'm going into the Indian Desert," I explained.

"Well *and* good," said he. "You'll be changing at Marwar Junction to get into Jodhpore territory—you must do that—and he'll be coming through Marwar Junction in the early morning of the 24th by the Bombay Mail. Can you be at Marwar Junction on that time? 'Twon't be inconveniencing you because I know that there's precious few pickings to be got out of these Central India States—even though you pretend to be correspondent of the *Backwoodsman.*"

"Have you ever tried that trick?" I asked.

"Again and again, but the Residents find you out, and then you get escorted to the Border before you've time to get your knife into them. But about my friend here. I *must* give him a word o' mouth to tell him what's come to me or else he won't know where to go. I would take it more than kind of you if you was to come out of Central India in time to catch him at Marwar Junction, and say to him:—'He has gone South for the week.' He'll know what that means. He's a big man with a red beard, and great swell he is. You'll find him sleeping like a gentleman with all his luggage round him in a Second-class compartment. But don't you be afraid. Slip down the window, and say:—'He has gone South for the week,' and he'll tumble. It's only cutting your time of stay in those parts

by two days. I ask you as a stranger—going to the West,"
he said, with emphasis.

"Where have *you* come from?" said I.

"From the East," said he, "and I am hoping that you
will give him the message on the Square—for the sake of
my Mother as well as your own."

Englishmen are not usually softened by appeals to the
memory of their mothers, but for certain reasons, which
will be fully apparent, I saw fit to agree.

"It's more than a little matter," said he, "and that's
why I ask you to do it—and now I know that I can de-
pend on you doing it. A Second-class carriage at Marwar
Junction, and a red-haired man asleep in it. You'll be
sure to remember. I get out at the next station, and I
must hold on there till he comes or sends me what I want."

"I'll give the message if I catch him," I said, "and for
the sake of your Mother as well as mine I'll give you a
word of advice. Don't try to run the Central India States
just now as the correspondent of the *Backwoodsman*.
There's a real one knocking about here, and it might lead
to trouble."

"Thank you," said he, simply, "and when will the swine
be gone? I can't starve because he's ruining my work. I
wanted to get hold of the Degumber Rajah down here
about his father's widow, and give him a jump."

"What did he do to his father's widow, then?"

"Filled her up with red pepper and slippered her to
death as she hung from a beam. I found that out myself
and I'm the only man that would dare going into the State
to get hush-money for it. They'll try to poison me, same
as they did in Chortumna when I went on the loot there.

But you'll give the man at Marwar Junction my message?"

He got out at a little roadside station, and I reflected. I had heard, more than once, of men personating correspondents of newspapers and bleeding small Native States with threats of exposure, but I had never met any of the caste before. They lead a hard life, and generally die with great suddenness. The Native States have a wholesome horror of English newspapers, which throw light on their peculiar methods of government, and do their best to choke correspondents with champagne, or drive them out of their mind with four-in-hand barouches. They do not understand that nobody cares a straw for the internal administration of Native States so long as oppression and crime are kept within decent limits, and the ruler is not drugged, drunk, or diseased from one end of the year to the other. Native States were created by Providence in order to supply picturesque scenery, tigers, and tall-writing. They are the dark places of the earth, full of unimaginable cruelty, touching the Railway and the Telegraph on one side, and, on the other, the days of Harun-al-Raschid. When I left the train I did business with divers Kings, and in eight days passed through many changes of life. Sometimes I wore dress-clothes and consorted with Princes and Politicals, drinking from crystal and eating from silver. Sometimes I lay out upon the ground and devoured what I could get, from a plate made of a flapjack, and drank the running water, and slept under the same rug as my servant. It was all in the day's work.

Then I headed for the Great Indian Desert upon the proper date, as I had promised, and the night Mail set me down at Marwar Junction, where a funny little, happy-go-lucky, native-managed railway runs to Jodhpore. The Bombay Mail from Delhi makes a short halt at Marwar. She arrived as I got in, and I had just time to hurry to her platform and go down the carriages. There was only one Second-class on the train. I slipped the window and looked down upon a flaming red beard, half covered by a railway rug. That was my man, fast asleep, and I dug him gently in the ribs. He woke with a grunt and I saw his face in the light of the lamps. It was a great and shining face.

"Tickets again?" said he.

"No," said I. "I am to tell you that he is gone South for the week. He is gone South for the week!"

The train had begun to move out. The red man rubbed his eyes. "He has gone South for the week," he repeated. "Now that's just like his impidence. Did he say that I was to give you anything?—'Cause I won't."

"He didn't," I said, and dropped away, and watched the red lights die out in the dark. It was horribly cold because the wind was blowing off the sands. I climbed into my own train—not an Intermediate Carriage this time—and went to sleep.

If the man with the beard had given me a rupee I should have kept it as a memento of a rather curious affair. But the consciousness of having done my duty was my only reward.

Later on I reflected that two gentlemen like my friends could not do any good if they foregathered and personated correspondents of newspapers, and might, if they "stuck up" one of the little rat-trap states of Central India or Southern Rajputana, get themselves into serious difficulties.

I therefore took some trouble to describe them as accurately as I could remember to people who would be interested in deporting them: and succeeded, so I was later informed, in having them headed back from the Degumber borders.

Then I became respectable, and returned to an Office where there were no Kings and no incidents except the daily manufacture of a newspaper. A newspaper office seems to attract every conceivable sort of person, to the prejudice of discipline. Zenana-mission ladies arrive and beg that the Editor will instantly abandon all his duties to describe a Christian prizegiving in a back-slum of a perfectly inaccessible village; Colonels who have been overpassed for commands sit down and sketch the outline of a series of ten, twelve, or twenty-four leading articles on Seniority *versus* Selection; missionaries wish to know why they have not been permitted to escape from their regular vehicles of abuse and swear at a brother-missionary under special patronage of the editorial We; stranded theatrical companies troop up to explain that they cannot pay for their advertisements, but on their return from New Zealand or Tahiti will do so with interest; inventors of patent punkah-pulling machines, carriage couplings and unbreakable swords and axle-trees call with specifications in their pockets and hours at their disposal; tea companies enter and elaborate their prospectuses with the office pens; secretaries of ball-committees clamor to have the glories of their last dance more fully expounded; strange ladies rustle in and say:—"I want a hundred lady's cards printed *at once*, please," which is manifestly part of an Editor's duty; and every dissolute ruffian that ever tramped the Grand

Trunk Road makes it his business to ask for employment as a proof-reader. And, all the time, the telephone-bell is ringing madly, and Kings are being killed on the Continent, and Empires are saying—"You're another," and Mister Gladstone is calling down brimstone upon the British Dominions, and the little black copy-boys are whining, *"kaa-pi chay-ha-yeh"* (copy wanted) like tired bees, and most of the paper is as blank as Modred's shield.

But that is the amusing part of the year. There are other six months wherein none ever come to call, and the thermometer walks inch by inch up to the top of the glass, and the office is darkened to just above reading-light, and the press-machines are red-hot of touch, and nobody writes anything but accounts of amusements in the Hill-stations or obituary notices. Then the telephone becomes a tinkling terror, because it tells you of the sudden deaths of men and women that you knew intimately, and the prickly-heat covers you as with a garment, and you sit down and write:—"A slight increase of sickness is reported from the Khuda Janta Khan District. The outbreak is purely sporadic in its nature, and, thanks to the energetic efforts of the District authorities, is now almost at an end. It is, however, with deep regret we record the death, etc."

Then the sickness really breaks out, and the less recording and reporting the better for the peace of the subscribers. But the Empires and the Kings continue to divert themselves as selfishly as before, and the Foreman thinks that a daily paper really ought to come out once in twenty-four hours, and all the people at the Hill-stations in the middle of their amusements say:—"Good gracious! Why can't the paper be sparkling? I'm sure there's plenty going on up here."

That is the dark half of the moon, and, as the advertisements say, "must be experienced to be appreciated."

It was in that season, and a remarkably evil season, that the paper began running the last issue of the week on Saturday night, which is to say Sunday morning, after the custom of a London paper. This was a great convenience, for immediately after the paper was put to bed, the dawn would lower the thermometer from 96° to almost 84° for half an hour, and in that chill—you have no idea how cold is 84° on the grass until you begin to pray for it—a very tired man could set off to sleep ere the heat roused him.

One Saturday night it was my pleasant duty to put the paper to bed alone. A King or courtier or a courtesan or a community was going to die or get a new Constitution, or do something that was important on the other side of the world, and the paper was to be held open till the latest possible minute in order to catch the telegram. It was a pitchy black night, as stifling as a June night can be, and the *loo*, the red-hot wind from the westward, was booming among the tinder-dry trees and pretending that the rain was on its heels. Now and again a spot of almost boiling water would fall on the dust with the flop of a frog, but all our weary world knew that was only pretence. It was a shade cooler in the press-room than the office, so I sat there, while the type ticked and clicked, and the nightjars hooted at the windows, and the all but naked compositors wiped the sweat from their foreheads and called for water. The thing that was keeping us back, whatever it was, would not come off, though the *loo* dropped and the last type was set, and the whole round earth stood still in the choking heat, with its finger on its lip, to wait the event. I drowsed, and wondered whether the telegraph was a blessing, and whether this dying man, or struggling people, was aware of the inconvenience the delay was causing. There was no special reason beyond the heat and worry to make tension, but, as the clock hands crept up to three o'clock and the machines spun their fly-wheels two and three times to see that all was in order, before I said the word that would set them off, I could have shrieked aloud.

Then the roar and rattle of the wheels shivered the quiet into little bits. I rose to go away, but two men in white clothes stood in front of me. The first one said:—"It's him!" The second said:—"So it is!" And they both laughed almost as loudly as the machinery roared, and mopped their foreheads. "We see there was a light burning across the road and we were sleeping in that ditch there for coolness, and I said to my friend here, 'The office is open. Let's come along and speak to him as turned us back from the Degumber State,'" said the smaller of the two. He was the man I had met in the Mhow train, and his fellow was the red-bearded man of Marwar Junction. There was no mistaking the eyebrows of the one or the beard of the other.

I was not pleased, because I wished to go to sleep, not to squabble with loafers. "What do you want?" I asked.

"Half an hour's talk with you cool and comfortable in the office," said the red-bearded man. "We'd *like* some drink—the Contrack doesn't begin yet, Peachey, so you needn't look—but what we really want is advice. We don't want money. We ask you as a favor, because you did us a bad turn about Degumber."

I led from the press-room to the stifling office with the maps on the walls, and the red-haired man rubbed his hands. "That's something like," said he. "This was the proper shop to come to. Now, Sir, let me introduce to you Brother Peachey Carnehan, that's him, and Brother Daniel Dravot, that is *me*, and the less said about our professions the better, for we have been most things in our time. Soldier, sailor, compositor, photographer, proof-reader, street-preacher, and correspondents of the *Backwoodsman* when we thought the paper wanted one. Carnehan is sober, and so am I. Look at us first and see that's sure. It will save you cutting into my talk. We'll take one of your cigars apiece, and you shall see us light."

I watched the test. The men were absolutely sober, so I gave them each a tepid peg.

"Well *and* good," said Carnehan of the eyebrows, wiping the froth from his moustache. "Let me talk now, Dan. We have been all over India, mostly on foot. We have been boiler-fitters, engine-drivers, petty contractors, and all that, and we have decided that India isn't big enough for such as us."

They certainly were too big for the office. Dravot's beard seemed to fill half the room and Carnehan's shoulders the other half, as they sat on the big table. Carnehan continued:—"The country isn't half worked out because they that governs it won't let you touch it. They spend all their blessed time in governing it, and you can't lift a spade, nor chip a rock, nor look for oil, nor anything like that without all the Government saying—'Leave it alone and let us govern.' Therefore, such as it is, we will let it alone, and go away to some other place where a man isn't crowded and can come to his own. We are not little men, and there is nothing that we are afraid of except Drink, and we have signed a Contrack on that. *Therefore, we are going away to be Kings.*"

"Kings in our own right," muttered Dravot.

"Yes, of course," I said. "You've been tramping in the sun, and it's a very warm night, and hadn't you better sleep over the notion? Come to-morrow."

"Neither drunk nor sun-stroke," said Dravot. "We have slept over the notion half a year, and require to see Books and Atlases, and we have decided that there is only one place now in the world that two strong men can Sar-a-*whack*. They call it Kafiristan. By my reckoning it's the top right-hand corner of Afghanistan, not more than three hundred miles from Peshawur. They have two and thirty heathen idols there, and we'll be the thirty-third. It's a mountaineous country, and the women of those parts are very beautiful."

"But that is provided against in the Contrack," said Carnehan. "Neither Women nor Liqu-or, Daniel."

"And that's all we know, except that no one has gone there, and they fight, and in any place where they fight a man who knows how to drill men can always be a King. We shall go to those parts and say to any King we find— 'D'you want to vanquish your foes?' and we will show him how to drill men; for that we know better than anything else. Then we will subvert that King and seize his Throne and establish a Dy-nasty."

"You'll be cut to pieces before you're fifty miles across

the Border," I said. "You have to travel through Afghanistan to get to that country. It's one mass of mountains and peaks and glaciers, and no Englishman has been through it. The people are utter brutes, and even if you reached them you couldn't do anything."

"That's more like," said Carnehan. "If you could think us a little more mad we would be more pleased. We have come to you to know about this country, to read a book about it, and to be shown maps. We want you to tell us that we are fools and to show us your books." He turned to the bookcases.

"Are you at all in earnest?" I said.

"A little," said Dravot, sweetly. "As big a map as you have got, even if it's all blank where Kafiristan is, and any books you've got. We can read, though we aren't very educated."

I uncased the big thirty-two-miles-to-the-inch map of India, and two smaller Frontier maps, hauled down volume INF-KAN of the *Encyclopædia Brittanica*, and the men consulted them.

"See here!" said Dravot, his thumb on the map. "Up to Jagdallak, Peachey and me know the road. We was there with Roberts's Army. We'll have to turn off to the right at Jagdallak through Laghmann territory. Then we get among the hills—fourteen thousand feet—fifteen thousand—it will be cold work there, but it don't look very far on the map."

I handed him Wood on the *Sources of the Oxus*. Carnehan was deep in the *Encyclopædia*.

"They're a mixed lot," said Dravot, reflectively; "and it won't help us to know the names of their tribes. The more tribes the more they'll fight, and the better for us. From Jagdallak to Ashang. H'mm!"

"But all the information about the country is as sketchy and inaccurate as can be," I protested. "No one knows anything about it really. Here's the file of the *United Services' Institute*. Read what Bellew says."

"Blow Bellew!" said Carnehan. "Dan, they're an all-fired lot of heathens, but this book here says they think they're related to us English."

I smoked while the men pored over *Raverty, Wood*, the maps and the *Encyclopædia*.

"There is no use your waiting," said Dravot, politely. "It's about four o'clock now. We'll go before six o'clock if you want to sleep, and we won't steal any of the papers. Don't you sit up. We're two harmless lunatics, and if you come, to-morrow evening, down to the Serai we'll say good-bye to you."

"You *are* two fools," I answered. "You'll be turned back at the Frontier or cut up the minute you set foot in Afghanistan. Do you want any money or a recommendation down-country? I can help you to the chance of work next week."

"Next week we shall be hard at work ourselves, thank you," said Dravot. "It isn't so easy being a King as it looks. When we've got our Kingdom in going order we'll let you know, and you can come up and help us to govern it."

"Would two lunatics make a Contrack like that?" said Carnehan, with subdued pride, showing me a greasy half-sheet of note-paper on which was written the following. I copied it, then and there, as a curiosity:

This Contract between me and you persuing witnesseth in the name of God—Amen and so forth.

(One) *That me and you will settle this matter together: i. e., to be Kings of Kafiristan.*

(Two) *That you and me will not, while this matter is being settled, look at any Liquor, nor any Woman, black, white or brown, so as to get mixed up with one or the other harmful.*

(Three) *That we conduct ourselves with dignity and discretion, and if one of us gets into trouble the other will stay by him.*

Signed by you and me this day.

Peachey Taliaferro Carnehan.
Daniel Dravot.
Both Gentlemen at Large.

"There was no need for the last article," said Carnehan, blushing modestly; "but it looks regular. Now you know the sort of men that loafers are—we *are* loafers, Dan, until we get out of India— and *do* you think that we would sign a Contrack like that unless we was in earnest? We have kept away from the two things that make life worth having."

"You won't enjoy your lives much longer if you are going to try this idiotic adventure. Don't set the office on fire," I said, "and go away before nine o'clock."

I left them still poring over the maps and making notes on the back of the "Contrack." "Be sure to come down to the Serai to-morrow," were their parting words.

The Kumharsen Serai is the great four-square sink of humanity where the strings of camels and horses from the

North load and unload. All the nationalities of Central Asia may be found there, and most of the folk of India proper. Balkh and Bokhara there meet Bengal and Bombay, and try to draw eye-teeth. You can buy ponies, turquoises, Persian pussy-cats, saddlebags, fat-tailed sheep and musk in the Kumharsen Serai, and get many strange things for nothing. In the afternoon I went down there to see whether my friends intended to keep their word or were lying about drunk.

A priest attired in fragments of ribbons and rags stalked up to me, gravely twisting a child's paper whirligig. Behind him was his servant bending under the load of a crate of mud toys. The two were loading up two camels, and the inhabitants of the Serai watched them with shrieks of laughter.

"The priest is mad," said a horse-dealer to me. "He is going up to Kabul to sell toys to the Amir. He will either be raised to honor or have his head cut off. He came in here this morning and has been behaving madly ever since."

"The witless are under the protection of God," stammered a flat-cheeked Usbeg in broken Hindi. "They foretell future events."

"Would they could have foretold that my caravan would have been cut up by the Shinwaris almost within shadow of the Pass!" grunted the Eusufzai agent of a Rajputana trading-house whose goods had been feloniously diverted into the hands of other robbers just across the Border, and whose misfortunes were the laughing-stock of the bazar. "Ohé, priest, whence come you and whither do you go?"

"From Roum have I come," shouted the priest, waving

his whirligig; "from Roum, blown by the breath of a hundred devils across the sea! O thieves, robbers, liars, the blessing of Pir Khan on pigs, dogs, and perjurers! Who will take the Protected of God to the North to sell charms that are never still to the Amir? The camels shall not gall, the sons shall not fall sick, and the wives shall remain faithful while they are away, of the men who give me place in their caravan. Who will assist me to slipper the King of the Roos with a golden slipper with a silver heel? The protection of Pir Khan be upon his labors!" He spread out the skirts of his gabardine and pirouetted between the lines of tethered horses.

"There starts a caravan from Peshawur to Kabul in twenty days, *Huzrut*," said the Eusufzai trader. "My camels go therewith. Do thou also go and bring us good-luck."

"I will go even now!" shouted the priest. "I will depart upon my winged camels, and be at Peshawur in a day! Ho! Hazar Mir Khan," he yelled to his servant, "drive out the camels, but let me first mount my own."

He leaped on the back of his beast as it knelt, and, turning round to me, cried:—"Come thou also, Sahib, a little along the road, and I will sell thee a charm—an amulet that shall make thee King of Kafiristan."

Then the light broke upon me, and I followed the two camels out of the Serai till we reached open road and the priest halted.

"What d' you think o' that?" said he in English. "Carnehan can't talk their patter, so I've made him my servant. He makes a handsome servant. 'Tisn't for nothing that I've been knocking about the country for fourteen years. Didn't

I do that talk neat? We'll hitch on to a caravan at Peshawur till we get to Jagdallak, and then we'll see if we can get donkeys for our camels, and strike into Kafiristan. Whirligigs for the Amir, O Lor! Put your hand under the camel-bags and tell me what you feel."

I felt the butt of a Martini, and another and another.

"Twenty of 'em," said Dravot, placidly. "Twenty of 'em, and ammunition to correspond, under the whirligigs and the mud dolls."

"Heaven help you if you are caught with those things!" I said. "A Martini is worth her weight in silver among the Pathans."

"Fifteen hundred rupees of capital—every rupee we could beg, borrow, or steal—are invested on these two camels," said Dravot. "We won't get caught. We're going through the Khaiber with a regular caravan. Who'd touch a poor mad priest?"

"Have you got everything you want?" I asked, overcome with astonishment.

"Not yet, but we shall soon. Give us a memento of your kindness, *Brother.* You did me a service yesterday, and that time in Marwar. Half my Kingdom shall you have, as the saying is." I slipped a small charm compass from my watch-chain and handed it up to the priest.

"Good-bye," said Dravot, giving me hand cautiously. "It's the last time we'll shake hands with an Englishman these many days. Shake hands with him, Carnehan," he cried, as the second camel passed me.

Carnehan leaned down and shook hands. Then the camels passed away along the dusty road, and I was left alone to wonder. My eye could detect no failure in the disguises. The scene in Serai attested that they were complete to the native mind. There was just the chance, therefore, that Carnehan and Dravot would be able to wander through Afghanistan without detection. But, beyond, they would find death, certain and awful death.

Ten days later a native friend of mine, giving me the news of the day from Peshawur, wound up his letter with: —"There has been much laughter here on account of a certain mad priest who is going in his estimation to sell petty gauds and insignificant trinkets which he ascribes as great charms to H. H. the Amir of Bokhara. He passed through Peshawur and associated himself to the Second Summer caravan that goes to Kabul. The merchants are pleased because through superstition they imagine that such mad fellows bring good-fortune."

The two, then, were beyond the Border. I would have prayed for them, but, that night, a real King died in Europe, and demanded an obituary notice.

*   *   *   *   *   *   *   *   *

The wheel of the world swings through the same phases again and again. Summer passed and winter thereafter, and came and passed again. The daily paper continued and I with it, and upon the third summer there fell a hot night, a night-issue, and a strained waiting for something to be telegraphed from the other side of the world, exactly as had happened before. A few great men had died in the past two years, the machines worked with more clatter, and some of the trees in the Office garden were a few feet taller. But that was all the difference.

I passed over to the press-room, and went through just such a scene as I have already described. The nervous tension was stronger than it had been two years before, and I felt the heat more acutely. At three o'clock I cried, "Print off," and turned to go, when there crept to my chair what was left of a man. He was bent into a circle, his head was sunk between his shoulders, and he moved his feet one over the other like a bear. I could hardly see whether he walked or crawled—this rag-wrapped, whining cripple who addressed me by name, crying that he was come back. "Can you give me a drink?" he whimpered. "For the Lord's sake, give me a drink!"

I went back to the office, the man following with groans of pain, and I turned up the lamp.

"Don't you know me?" he gasped, dropping into a chair, and he turned his drawn face, surmounted by a shock of grey hair, to the light.

I looked at him intently. Once before had I seen eyebrows that met over the nose in an inch-broad black band, but for the life of me I could not tell where.

"I don't know you," I said, handing him the whiskey. "What can I do for you?"

He took a gulp of the spirit raw, and shivered in spite of the suffocating heat.

"I've come back," he repeated; "and I was the King of Kafiristan—me and Dravot—crowned Kings we was! In this office we settled it—you setting there and giving us the books. I am Peachey—Peachey Taliaferro Carnehan, and you've been setting here ever since—O Lord!"

I was more than a little astonished, and expressed my feelings accordingly.

"It's true," said Carnehan, with a dry cackle, nursing his feet, which were wrapped in rags. "True as gospel.

Kings we were, with crowns upon our heads—me and Dravot—poor Dan—oh, poor, poor Dan, that would never take advice, not though I begged of him!"

"Take the whiskey," I said, "and take your own time. Tell me all you can recollect of everything from beginning to end. You got across the border on your camels, Dravot dressed as a mad priest and you his servant. Do you remember that?"

"I ain't mad—yet, but I shall be that way soon. Of course I remember. Keep looking at me, or maybe my words will go all to pieces. Keep looking at me in my eyes and don't say anything."

I leaned forward and looked into his face as steadily as I could. He dropped one hand upon the table and I grasped it by the wrist. It was twisted like a bird's claw, and upon the back was a ragged, red, diamond-shaped scar.

"No, don't look there. Look at *me*," said Carnehan.

"That comes afterward, but for the Lord's sake don't distrack me. We left with that caravan, me and Dravot playing all sorts of antics to amuse the people we were with. Dravot used to make us laugh in the evenings when all the people were cooking their dinners—cooking their dinners, and . . . what did they do then? They lit little fires with sparks that went into Dravot's beard, and we all laughed—fit to die. Little red fires they was, going into Dravot's big red beard—so funny." His eyes left mine and he smiled foolishly.

"You went as far as Jagdallak with that caravan," I said, at a venture, "after you had lit those fires. To Jagdallak, where you turned off to try to get into Kafiristan."

"No, we didn't neither. What are you talking about? We turned off before Jagdallak, because we heard the roads was good. But they wasn't good enough for our two camels—mine and Dravot's. When we left the caravan, Dravot took off all his clothes and mine too, and said we would be heathen, because the Kafirs didn't allow Mohammedans to talk to them. So we dressed betwixt and between, and such a sight as Daniel Dravot I never saw yet nor expect to see again. He burned half his beard, and slung a sheep-skin over his shoulder, and shaved his head into patterns. He shaved mine, too, and made me wear outrageous things to look like a heathen. That was in a most mountaineous country, and our camels couldn't go along any more because of the mountains. They were tall and black, and coming home I saw them fight like wild goats—there are lots of goats in Kafiristan. And these mountains, they never keep still, no more than the goats. Always fighting they are, and don't let you sleep at night."

"Take some more whiskey," I said, very slowly. "What did you and Daniel Dravot do when the camels could go no further because of the rough roads that led into Kafiristan?"

"What did which do? There was a party called Peachey Taliaferro Carnehan that was with Dravot. Shall I tell you about him? He died out there in the cold. Slap from the bridge fell old Peachey, turning and twisting in the air like a penny whirligig that you can sell to the Amir.—No; they was two for three ha'pence, those whirligigs, or I am much mistaken and woful sore. And then these camels were no use, and Peachey said to Dravot—'For the Lord's sake, let's get out of this before our heads are chopped off,' and with that they killed the camels all among the mountains, not having anything in particular to eat, but first they took off the boxes with the guns and the ammunition, till two men came along driving four mules. Dravot up and dances in front of them, singing—'Sell me four mules.' Says the first man,—'If you are rich enough to buy, you are rich enough to rob;' but before ever he could put his hand to his knife, Dravot breaks his neck over his knee, and the other party runs away. So Carnehan loaded the mules with the rifles that was taken off the camels, and together we starts forward into those bitter cold mountaineous parts, and never a road broader than the back of your hand."

He paused for a moment, while I asked him if he could remember the nature of the country through which he had journeyed.

"I am telling you as straight as I can, but my head isn't as good as it might be. They drove nails through it to make me hear better how Dravot died. The country was mountaineous and the mules were most contrary, and the inhabitants was dispersed and solitary. They went up and up, and down and down, and that other party, Carnehan, was imploring of Dravot not to sing and whistle so loud, for fear of bringing down the tremenjus avalanches. But Dravot says that if a King couldn't sing it wasn't worth being King, and whacked the mules over the rump, and never took no heed for ten cold days. We came to a big level valley all among the mountains, and the mules were near dead, so we killed them, not having anything in special for them or us to eat. We sat upon the boxes, and played odd and even with the cartridges that was jolted out.

"Then ten men with bows and arrows ran down that valley, chasing twenty men with bows and arrows, and the row was tremenjus. They was fair men—fairer than you or me—with yellow hair and remarkable well built. Says Dravot, unpacking the guns—'This is the beginning of the business. We'll fight for the ten men,' and with that he fires two rifles at the twenty men, and drops one of them at two hundred yards from the rock where he was sitting. The other men began to run, but Carnehan and Dravot sits on the boxes picking them off at all ranges, up and down the valley. Then we goes up to the ten men that had run across the snow too, and they fires a footy little arrow at us. Dravot he shoots above their heads and they all falls down flat. Then he walks over them and kicks them, and then he lifts them up and shakes hands all round to make them friendly like. He calls them and gives them the boxes to carry, and waves his hand for all the world as though he was King already. They takes the boxes and him across the valley and up the hill into a pine wood on the top, where there was half a dozen big stone idols. Dravot he goes to the biggest—a fellow they call Imbra—and lays a rifle and a cartridge at his feet, rubbing his nose respectful with his own nose, patting him on the head, and saluting in front of it. He turns around to the men and nods his head, and says,—'That's all right. I'm in the know too, and all these old jim-jams are my friends.' Then he opens his mouth and points down it, and when the first man brings him food, he says—'No'; and when the second man brings him food, he says—'No'; but when one of the old priests and the boss of the village brings him food, he says—'Yes'; very haughty, and eats it slow. That was how we came to our first village, without any trouble, just as though we had tumbled from the skies. But we tumbled from one of those damned rope-bridges, you see, and you couldn't expect a man to laugh much after that."

"Take some more whiskey and go on," I said. "That was the first village you came into. How did you get to be King?"

"I wasn't King," said Carnehan. "Dravot he was the King, and a handsome man he looked with the gold crown on his head and all. Him and the other party stayed in that village, and every morning Dravot sat by the side of old Imbra, and the people came and worshipped. That was Dravot's order. Then a lot of men came into the valley, and Carnehan and Dravot picks them off with the rifles before they knew where they was, and runs down into the valley and up again the other side, and finds another village, same as the first one, and the people all falls down flat on their faces, and Dravot says—'Now what is the trouble between you two villages?' and the people points to a woman, as fair as you or me, that was carried off, and Dravot takes her back to the first village and counts up the dead—eight there was. For each dead man Dravot pours a little milk on the ground and waves his arms like a whirligig and 'That's all right,' says he. Then he and Carnehan takes the big boss of each village by the arm and walks them down into the valley and shows them how to scratch a line with a spear right down the valley, and gives each a sod of turf from both sides o' the line. Then all the people comes down and shouts like the devil and all, and Dravot says,—'Go and dig the land, and be fruitful and multiply,' which they did, though they didn't understand. Then we asks the names of things in their lingo—bread and water and fire and idols and such, and Dravot leads the priest of each village up to the idol, and says he must sit there and judge the people, and if anything goes wrong he is to be shot.

"Next week they was all turning up the land in the valley as quiet as bees and much prettier, and the priests heard all the complaints and told Dravot in dumb show what it was about. 'That's just the beginning,' says Dravot. 'They think we're Gods.' He and Carnehan picks out twenty good men and shows them how to click off a rifle, and form fours, and advance in line, and they was very pleased to do so, and clever to see the hang of it. Then he takes out his pipe and his baccy-pouch and leaves one at one village and one at the other, and off we two goes to see what was to be done in the next valley. That was all rock, and there was a little village there, and Carnehan says,—'Send 'em to the old valley to plant,' and takes 'em there and gives 'em some land that wasn't took before. They were a poor lot, and we blooded 'em with a kid before letting 'em into the new Kingdom. That was to impress the people, and then they settled down quiet, and Carnehan went back to Dravot who had got into another valley, all snow and ice and most mountaineous. There was no people there and the Army got afraid, so Dravot shoots one of them, and goes on till he finds some people in a village, and the Army explains that unless the people wants to be killed they had better not shoot their little matchlocks; for they had matchlocks. We makes friends with the priest and I stays there alone with two of the Army, teaching the men how to drill, and a thundering big Chief comes across the snow with kettle-drums and horns twanging, because he heard there was a new God kicking about. Carnehan sights for the brown of the men half a mile across the snow and wings one of them. Then he sends a message to the Chief that, unless he wished to be killed, he must come and shake hands with me and leave his arms behind. The chief comes alone first, and Carnehan shakes hands with him and whirls his arms about, same as Dravot used, and very much surprised that Chief was, and strokes my eyebrows. Then Carnehan goes alone to the Chief, and asks him in dumb show if he had an enemy he hated. 'I have,' says the Chief. So Carnehan weeds out the pick of his men, and sets the two of the Army to show them drill and at the end of two weeks the men can manœuvre about as well as Volunteers. So he marches with the Chief to a great big plain on the top of a mountain, and the Chief's men rushes into a village and takes it; we three Martinis firing into the brown of the enemy. So we took that village too, and I gives the Chief a rag from my coat and says, 'Occupy till I come': which was scriptural. By way of a reminder, when me and the Army was eighteen hundred yards away, I drops a bullet near him standing on the snow, and all the people falls flat on their faces. Then I sends a letter to Dravot, wherever he be by land or by sea."

At the risk of throwing the creature out of train I interrupted,—"How could you write a letter up yonder?"

"The letter?—Oh!—The letter! Keep looking at me between the eyes, please. It was a string-talk letter, that we'd learned the way of it from a blind beggar in the Punjab."

I remember that there had once come to the office a blind man with a knotted twig and a piece of string which he wound round the twig according to some cypher of his own. He could, after the lapse of days or hours, repeat the sentence which he had reeled up. He had reduced the alphabet to eleven primitive sounds; and tried to teach me his method, but failed.

"I sent that letter to Dravot," said Carnehan; "and told him to come back because this Kingdom was growing too big for me to handle, and then I struck for the first valley, to see how the priests were working. They called the village we took along with the Chief, Bashkai, and the first village we took, Er-Heb. The priests at Er-Heb was doing all right, but they had a lot of pending cases about land to show me, and some men from another village had been firing arrows at night. I went out and looked for that village and fired four rounds at it from a thousand yards. That used all the cartridges I cared to spend, and I waited for Dravot, who had been away two or three months, and I kept my people quiet.

"One morning I heard the devil's own noise of drums and horns, and Dan Dravot marches down the hill with his Army and a tail of hundreds of men, and, which was the most amazing—a great gold crown on his head. 'My Gord, Carnehan,' says Daniel, 'this is a tremenjus business, and we've got the whole country as far as it's worth having. I am the son of Alexander by Queen Semiramis, and you're my younger brother and a God too! It's the biggest thing we've ever seen. I've been marching and fighting for six weeks with the Army, and every footy little village for fifty miles has come in rejoiceful; and more than that, I've got the key of the whole show, as you'll see, and I've got a crown for you! I told 'em to make two of 'em at a place called Shu, where the gold lies in the rock like suet in mutton. Gold I've seen, and turquoise I've kicked out of the cliffs, and there's garnets in the sands of the river, and here's a chunk of amber that a man brought me. Call up all the priests and, here, take your crown.'

"One of the men opens a black hair bag and I slips the crown on. It was too small and too heavy, but I wore it for the glory. Hammered gold it was—five pound weight, like a hoop of a barrel.

"'Peachey,' says Dravot, 'we don't want to fight no more. The Craft's the trick so help me!' and he brings forward that same Chief that I left at Bashkai—Billy Fish we called him afterward, because he was so like Billy Fish that drove the big tank-engine at Mach on the Bolan in the old days. 'Shake hands with him,' says Dravot, and I shook hands and nearly dropped, for Billy Fish gave me the Grip. I said nothing, but tried him with the Fellow Craft Grip. He answers, all right, and I tried the Master's Grip, but that was a slip. 'A Fellow Craft he is!' I says to Dan. 'Does he know the word?' 'He does,' says Dan, 'and all the priests know. It's a miracle! The Chiefs and the priests can work a Fellow Craft Lodge in a way that's very like ours, and they've cut the marks on the rocks, but they don't know the Third Degree, and they've come to find out. It's Gord's Truth. I've known these long years that the Afghans knew up to the Fellow Craft Degree, but this is a miracle. A God and a Grand-Master of the Craft am I, and a Lodge in the Third Degree I will open, and we'll raise the head priests and the Chiefs of the villages.'

" 'It's against all the law,' I says, 'holding a Lodge without warrant from any one; and we never held office in any Lodge.'

" 'It's a master-stroke of policy,' says Dravot. 'It means running a country as easy as a four-wheeled bogy on a down grade. We can't stop to inquire now, or they'll turn against us. I've forty Chiefs at my heel, and passed and raised according to their merits they shall be. Billet these men on the villages and see that we run up a Lodge of some kind. The temple of Imbra will do for the Lodge-room. The women must make aprons as you show them. I'll hold a levee of Chiefs to-night and Lodge to-morrow.'

"I was fair run off my legs, but I wasn't such a fool as not to see what a pull this Craft business gave us. I showed the priests' families how to make aprons of the degrees, but for Dravot's apron the blue border and marks was made of turquoise lumps on white hide, not cloth. We took a great square stone in the temple for the Master's chair, and little stones for the officers' chairs, and painted the black pavement with white squares, and did what we could to make things regular.

"At the levee which was held that night on the hillside with big bonfires, Dravot gives out that him and me were Gods and sons of Alexander, and Past Grand-Masters in the Craft, and was come to make Kafiristan a country where every man should eat in peace and drink in quiet, and specially obey us. Then the Chiefs come round to shake hands, and they was so hairy and white and fair it was just shaking hands with old friends. We gave them names according as they was like men we had known in India—Billy Fish, Holly Dilworth, Pikky Kergan that was Bazar-master when I was at Mhow, and so on and so on.

"*The* most amazing miracle was at Lodge next night. One of the old priests was watching us continuous, and I felt uneasy, for I knew we'd have to fudge the Ritual, and I didn't know what the men knew. The old priest was a stranger come in from beyond the village of Bashkai. The minute Dravot puts on the Master's apron that the girls had made for him, the priest fetches a whoop and a howl, and tries to overturn the stone that Dravot was sitting on. 'It's all up now,' I says. 'That comes of meddling with the Craft without warrant!' Dravot never winked an eye, not when ten priests took and tilted over the Grand-Master's chair—which was to say the stone of Imbra. The priest begins rubbing the bottom end of it to clear away the black dirt, and presently he shows all the other priests the Master's Mark, same as was on Dravot's apron, cut into the stone. Not even the priests of the temple of Imbra knew it was there. The old chap falls flat on his face at Dravot's feet and kisses 'em. 'Luck again,' says Dravot, across the Lodge to me, 'they say it's the missing Mark that no one could understand the why of. We're more than safe now.' Then he bangs the butt of his gun for a gavel and says:—'By virtue of the authority vested in me by my own right hand and the help of Peachey, I declare myself Grand-Master of all Freemasonry in Kafiristan in this the Mother Lodge o' the country, and King of Kafiristan equally with Peachey!' At that he puts on his crown and I puts on mine—I was do-

ing Senior Warden—and we opens the Lodge in most ample
form. It was a amazing miracle! The priests moved in
Lodge through the first two degrees almost without telling,
as if the memory was coming back to them. After that
Peachey and Dravot raised such as was worthy—high
priests and Chiefs of far-off villages. Billy Fish was the
the first, and I can tell you we scared the soul out of him.
It was not in any way according to Ritual, but it served
our turn. We didn't raise more than ten of the biggest
men because we didn't want to make the Degree common.
And they was clamoring to be raised.

"'In another six months,' says Dravot, 'we'll hold another Communication and see how you are working.' Then
he asks them about their villages, and learns that they
was fighting one against the other and were fair sick and
tired of it. And when they wasn't doing that they was
fighting with the Mohammedans. 'You can fight those
when they come into our country,' says Dravot. 'Tell off
every tenth man of your tribes for a Frontier guard, and
send two hundred at a time to this valley to be drilled.
Nobody is going to be shot or speared any more so long
as he does well, and I know that you won't cheat me because you're white people—sons of Alexander—and not
like common, black Mohammedans. You are *my* people and
by God,' says he, running off into English at the end—'I'll
make a damned fine Nation of you, or I'll die in the making!'

"I can't tell all we did for the next six months because
Dravot did a lot I couldn't see the hang of, and he learned
their lingo in a way I never could. My work was to help
the people plough, and now and again go out with some of

the Army and see what the other villages were doing, and make 'em throw rope-bridges across the ravines which cut up the country horrid. Dravot was very kind to me, but when he walked up and down in the pine wood pulling that bloody red beard of his with both fists I knew he was thinking plans I could not advise him about, and I just waited for orders.

"But Dravot never showed me disrespect before the people. They were afraid of me and the Army, but they loved Dan. He was the best of friends with the priests and the Chiefs; but any one could come across the hills with a complaint and Dravot would hear him out fair, and call four priests together and say what was to be done. He used to call in Billy Fish from Bashkai, and Pikky Kergan from Shu, and an old Chief we called Kafuzelum—it was like enough to his real name—and hold councils with 'em when there was any fighting to be done in small villages. That was his Council of War, and the four priests of Bashkai, Shu, Khawak, and Madora was his Privy Council. Between the lot of 'em they sent me, with forty men and twenty rifles, and sixty men carrying turquoises, into the Ghorband country to buy those hand-made Martini rifles, that come out of the Amir's workshops at Kabul, from one of the Amir's Herati regiments that would have sold the very teeth out of their mouths for turquoises.

"I stayed at Ghorband a month, and gave the Governor there the pick of my baskets for hush-money, and bribed the Colonel of the regiment some more, and, between the two and the tribes-people, we got more than a hundred hand-made Martinis, a hundred good Kohat Jezails that'll throw to six hundred yards, and forty man-loads of very bad ammunition for the rifles. I came back with what I had, and distributed 'em among the men that the Chiefs sent to me to drill. Dravot was too busy to attend to those things, but the old Army that we first made helped me, and we turned out five hundred men that could drill, and two hundred that knew how to hold arms pretty straight. Even those cork-screwed, hand-made guns was a miracle to them. Dravot talked big about powder-shops and factories, walking up and down in the pine wood when the winter was coming on.

"'I won't make a Nation,' says he. 'I'll make an Empire! These men aren't niggers; they're English! Look at their eyes—look at their mouths. Look at the way they stand up. They sit on chairs in their own houses. They're the Lost Tribes, or something like it, and they've grown to be English. I'll take a census in the spring if the priests don't get frightened. There must be a fair two million of 'em in these hills. The villages are full o' little children. Two million people—two hundred and fifty thousand fighting men—and all English! They only want the rifles and a little drilling. Two hundred and fifty thousand men, ready to cut in on Russia's right flank when she tries for India! Peachey, man,' he says, chewing his beard in great hunks, 'we shall be Emperors—Emperors of the Earth! Rajah Brooke will be a suckling to us. I'll treat with the Viceroy on equal terms. I'll ask him to send me twelve picked English—twelve that I know of—to help us govern a bit. There's Mackray, Sergeant-pensioner at Segowli—many's the good dinner he's given me, and his wife a pair of trousers. There's Donkin, the Warder of Tounghoo Jail; there's hundreds that I could lay my hand

on if I was in India. The Viceroy shall do it for me. I'll
send a man through in the spring for those men, and I'll
write for a dispensation from the Grand Lodge for what
I've done as Grand-Master. That—and all the Sniders
that'll be thrown out when the native troops in India take
up the Martini. They'll be worn smooth, but they'll do
for fighting in these hills. Twelve English, a hundred thous-
and Sniders run through the Amir's country in driblets—
I'd be content with twenty thousand in one year—and
we'd be an Empire. When everything was shipshape I'd
hand over the crown—this crown I'm wearing now—to
Queen Victoria on my knees, and she'd say: "Rise up, Sir
Daniel Dravot." Oh, it's big! It's big, I tell you! But
there's so much to be done in every place—Bashkai,
Khawak, Shu, and everywhere else.'

"'What is it?' I says. 'There are no more men coming
in to be drilled this autumn. Look at those fat, black
clouds. They're bringing the snow.'

"'It isn't that,' says Daniel, putting his hand very hard
on my shoulder; 'and I don't wish to say anything that's
against you, for no other living man would have followed
me and made me what I am as you have done. You're a
first-class Commander-in-Chief, and the people know you;
but—it's a big country, and somehow you can't help me,
Peachey, in the way I want to be helped.'

"'Go to your blasted priests, then!' I said, and I was
sorry when I made that remark, but it did hurt me sore
to find Daniel talking so superior when I'd drilled all the
men, and done all he told me.

"'Don't let's quarrel, Peachey,' says Daniel, without
cursing. 'You're a King too, and the half of this Kingdom

is yours; but can't you see, Peachey, we want cleverer men than us now—three or four of 'em, that we can scatter about for our Deputies. It's a hugeous great State, and I can't always tell the right thing to do, and I haven't time for all I want to do, and here's the winter coming on and all.' He put half his beard into his mouth, and it was as red as the gold of his crown.

" 'I'm sorry, Daniel,' says I. 'I've done all I could. I've drilled the men and shown the people how to stack their oats better; and I've brought in those tinware rifles from Ghorband—but I know what you're driving at. I take it Kings always feel oppressed that way.'

" 'There's another thing too,' says Dravot, walking up and down. 'The winter's coming and these people won't be giving much trouble, and if they do we can't move about. I want a wife.'

" 'For Gord's sake leave the women alone!' I says. 'We've both got all the work we can, though I *am* a fool. Remember the Contrack, and keep clear o' women.'

" 'The Contrack only lasted till such time as we was Kings; and Kings we have been these months past,' says Dravot, weighing his crown in his hand. 'You go get a wife too, Peachey—a nice, strappin', plump girl that'll keep you warm in the winter. They're prettier than English girls, and we can take the pick of 'em. Boil 'em once or twice in hot water, and they'll come as fair as chicken and ham.'

" 'Don't tempt me!' I says. 'I will not have any dealings with a woman not till we are a dam' side more settled than we are now. I've been doing the work o' two men, and you've been doing the work o' three. Let's lie off a bit, and see if we can get some better tobacco from Afghan country and run in some good liquor; but no women.'

" 'Who's talking o' *women*?' says Dravot. 'I said *wife*— a Queen to breed a King's son for the King. A Queen out of the strongest tribe, that'll make them your blood-brothers, and that'll lie by your side and tell you all the people thinks about you and their own affairs. That's what I want.'

" 'Do you remember that Bengali woman I kept at Mogul Serai when I was a plate-layer?' says I. 'A fat lot o' good she was to me. She taught me the lingo and one or two other things; but what happened? She ran away with the Station Master's servant and half my month's pay. Then she turned up at Dadur Junction in tow of a half-caste, and had the impidence to say I was her husband— all among the drivers in the running-shed!'

" 'We've done with that,' says Dravot. 'These women are whiter than you or me, and a Queen I will have for the winter months.'

" 'For the last time o' asking, Dan, do *not*,' I says. 'It'll only bring us harm. The Bible says that Kings ain't to waste their strength on women, 'specially when they've got a new raw Kingdom to work over.'

" 'For the last time of answering I will,' said Dravot, and he went away through the pine-trees looking like a big red devil. The low sun hit his crown and beard on one side and the two blazed like hot coals.

"But getting a wife was not as easy as Dan thought. He put it before the Council, and there was no answer till Billy Fish said that he'd better ask the girls. Dravot damned them all round. 'What's wrong with me?' he

shouts, standing by the idol Imbra. Am I a dog or am I
not enough of a man for your wenches? Haven't I put the
shadow of my hand over this country? Who stopped the
last Afghan raid? It was me really, but Dravot was too
angry to remember. 'Who brought your guns? Who re-
paired the bridges? Who's the Grand-Master of the sign
cut in the stone?' and he thumped his hand on the block
that he used to sit on in Lodge, and at Council, which
opened like Lodge always. Billy Fish said nothing and no
more did the others. 'Keep your hair on, Dan,' said I;
'and ask the girls. That's how it's done at Home, and
these people are quite English.'

" 'The marriage of the King is a matter of State,' says
Dan, in a white-hot rage, for he could feel, I hope, that he
was going against his better mind. He walked out of the
Council-room, and the others sat still, looking at the
ground.

" 'Billy Fish,' says I to the Chief of Bashkai, 'what's the
difficulty here? A straight answer to a true friend.' 'You
know,' says Billy Fish. 'How should a man tell you who
know everything? How can daughters of men marry Gods
or Devils? It's not proper.'

"I remembered something like that in the Bible; but if,
after seeing us as long as they had, they still believed we
were Gods, it wasn't for me to undeceive them.

" 'A God can do anything,' says I. 'If the King is fond
of a girl he'll not let her die.' 'She'll have to,' said Billy
Fish. 'There are all sorts of Gods and Devils in these
mountains, and now and again a girl marries one of them
and isn't seen any more. Besides, you two know the Mark
cut in the stone. Only the Gods know that. We thought

you were men till you showed the sign of the Master.'

"I wished then that we had explained about the loss of the genuine secrets of a Master-Mason at the first go-off; but I said nothing. All that night there was a blowing of horns in a little dark temple half-way down the hill, and I heard a girl crying fit to die. One of the priests told us that she was being prepared to marry the King.

" 'I'll have no nonsense of that kind,' says Dan. 'I don't want to interfere wiith your customs, but I'll take my own wife.' 'The girl's a little bit afraid,' says the priest. 'She thinks she's going to die, and they are aheartening of her up down in the temple.'

" 'Hearten her very tender, then,' says Dravot, 'or I'll hearten you with the butt of a gun so that you'll never want to be heartened again.' He licked his lips, did Dan, and stayed up walking about more than half the night, thinking of the wife that he was going to get in the morning. I wasn't any means comfortable, for I knew that dealings with a woman in foreign parts, though you was a crowned King twenty times over, could not but be risky. I got up very early in the morning while Dravot was asleep, and I saw the priests talking together in whispers, and the Chiefs talking together too, and they looked at me out of the corners of their eyes.

" 'What is up, Fish?' I says to the Bashkai man, who was wrapped up in his furs and looking splendid to behold.

" 'I can't rightly say,' says he; 'but if you can induce the King to drop all this nonsense about marriage you'll be doing him and me and yourself a great service.'

" 'That I do believe,' says I. 'But sure, you know, Billy, as well as me, having fought against and for us, that the

King and me are nothing more than two of the finest men that God Almighty ever made. Nothing more, I do assure you.'

"'That may be,' says Billy Fish, 'and yet I should be sorry if it was.' He sinks his head upon his great fur cloak for a minute and thinks. 'King,' says he, 'be you man or God or Devil, I'll stick by you to-day. I have twenty of my men with me, and they will follow me. We'll go to Bashkai until the storm blows over.'

"A little snow had fallen in the night, and everything was white except the greasy fat clouds that blew down and down from the north. Dravot came out with his crown on his head, swinging his arms and stamping his feet, and looking more pleased than Punch.

"'For the last time, drop it, Dan,' says I, in a whisper. 'Billy Fish here says that there will be a row.'

"'A row among my people!' says Dravot. 'Not much. Peachey, you're a fool not to get a wife too. Where's the girl?' says he, with a voice as loud as the braying of a jackass. 'Call up all the Chiefs and priests, and let the Emperor see if his wife suits him.'

"There was no need to call any one. They were all there leaning on their guns and spears round the clearing in the centre of the pine wood. A deputation of priests went down to the little temple to bring up the girl, and the horns blew up fit to wake the dead. Billy Fish saunters round and gets so close to Daniel as he could, and behind him stood his twenty men with matchlocks. Not a man of them under six feet. I was next to Dravot, and behind me was twenty men of the regular Army. Up comes the girl, and a strapping wench she was, covered with silver and turquoises but white as death, and looking back every minute at the priests.

"'She'll do,' said Dan, looking her over. 'What's to be afraid of, lass? Come and kiss me.' He puts his arm round her. She shuts her eyes, gives a bit of a squeak, and down goes her face in the side of Dan's flaming red beard.

"'The slut's bitten me!' says he, clapping his hand to his neck, and, sure enough, his hand was red with blood. Billy Fish and two of his matchlock-men catches hold of Dan by the shoulders and drags him into the Bashkai lot, while the priests howl in their lingo,—'Neither God nor Devil but a man!' I was all taken aback, for a priest cut at me in front, and the Army behind began firing into the Bashkai men.

"'God A-mighty!' says Dan. 'What is the meaning o' this?'

"'Come back! Come away!' says Billy Fish. 'Ruin and Mutiny is the matter. We'll break for Bashkai if we can.'

"I tried to give some sort of orders to my men—the men o' the regular Army—but it was no use, so I fired into the brown of 'em with an English Martini and drilled three beggars in a line. The valley was full of shouting, howling creatures, and every soul was shrieking, 'Not a God nor a Devil but only a man!' The Bashkai troops stuck to Billy Fish all they were worth, but their matchlocks wasn't half as good as the Kabul breech-loaders, and four of them dropped. Dan was bellowing like a bull, for he was very wrathy; and Billy Fish had a hard job to prevent him running out at the crowd.

"'We can't stand,' says Billy Fish. 'Make a run for it

down the valley! The whole place is against us.' The matchlock-men ran, and we went down the valley in spite of Dravot's protestations. He was swearing horribly and crying out that he was a King. The priests rolled great stones on us, and the regular Army fired hard, and there wasn't more than six men, not counting Dan, Billy Fish, and Me, that came down to the bottom of the valley alive.

"Then they stopped firing and the horns in the temple blew again. 'Come away—for God's sake come away!' says Billy Fish. 'They'll send runners out to all the villages before ever we get to Bashkai. I can protect you there, but I can't do anything now.'

"My own notion is that Dan began to go mad in his head from that hour. He stared up and down like a stuck pig. Then he was all for walking back alone and killing the priests with his bare hands; which he could have done. 'An Emperor am I,' says Daniel, 'and next year I shall be a Knight of the Queen.'

"'All right, Dan,' says I; 'but come along now while there's time.'

"'It's your fault,' says he, 'for not looking after your Army better. There was mutiny in the midst, and you didn't know—you damned engine-driving, plate-laying, missionary's-pass-hunting hound!' He sat upon a rock and called me every foul name he could lay tongue to. I was too heart-sick to care, though it was all his foolishness that brought the smash.

"'I'm sorry, Dan,' says I, 'but there's no accounting for natives. This business is our Fifty-Seven. Maybe we'll make something out of it yet, when we've got to Bashkai.'

" 'Let's get to Bashkai, then,' says Dan, 'and, by God when I come back here again I'll sweep the valley so there isn't a bug in a blanket left!'

"We walked all that day, and all that night Dan was stumping up and down on the snow, chewing his beard and muttering to himself.

" 'There's no hope o' getting clear,' said Billy Fish. 'The priests will have sent runners to the villages to say that you are only men. Why didn't you stick on as Gods till things was more settled? I'm a dead man,' says Billy Fish, and he throws himself down on the snow and begins to pray to his Gods.

"Next morning we was in a cruel bad country—all up and down, no level ground at all, and no food either. The six Bashkai men looked at Billy Fish hungry-wise as if they wanted to ask something, but they said never a word. At noon we came to the top of a flat mountain all covered with snow, and when we climbed up into it, behold, there was an Army in position waiting in the middle!

" 'The runners have been very quick,' says Billy Fish, with a little bit of a laugh. 'They are waiting for us.'

"Three or four men began to fire from the enemy's side, and a chance shot took Daniel in the calf of the leg. That brought him to his senses. He looks across the snow at the Army, and sees the rifles that we had brought into the country.

"We're done for," says he. 'They are Englishmen, these people,—and it's my blasted nonsense that has brought you to this. Get back, Billy Fish, and take your men away; you've done what you could, and now cut for it. Carnehan,' says he, 'shake hands with me and go along with

Billy. Maybe they won't kill you. I'll go and meet 'em alone. It's me that did it. Me, the King!'

" 'Go!' says I. 'Go to Hell, Dan! I'm with you here. Billy Fish, you clear out, and we two will meet those folk.'

" 'I'm a Chief,' says Billy Fish, quite quiet. 'I stay with you. My men can go.'

"The Bashkai fellows didn't wait for a second word but ran off, and Dan and Me and Billy Fish walked across to where the drums were drumming and the horns were horning. It was cold—awful cold. I've got that cold in the back of my head now. There's a lump of it there."

The punkah-coolies had gone to sleep. Two kerosene lamps were blazing in the office, and the perspiration poured down my face and splashed on the blotter as I leaned forward. Carnehan was shivering, and I feared that his mind might go. I wiped my face, took a fresh grip of the piteously mangled hands, and said:—"What happened after that?"

The momentary shift of my eyes had broken the clear current.

"What was you pleased to say?" whined Carnehan. "They took them without any sound. Not a little whisper all along the snow, not though the King knocked down the first man that set hand on him—not though old Peachey fired his last cartridge into the brown of 'em. Not a single solitary sound did those swines make. They just closed up tight, and I tell you their furs stunk. There was a man called Billy Fish, a good friend of us all, and they cut his throat, Sir, then and there, like a pig; and the King kicks up the bloody snow and says:—'We've had a dashed fine run for our money. What's coming next?' But Peachey,

Peachey Taliaferro, I tell you, Sir, in confidence as betwixt two friends, he lost his head, Sir. No, he didn't neither. The King lost his head, so he did, all along o' one of those cunning rope-bridges. Kindly let me have the paper-cutter, Sir. It tilted this way. They marched him a mile across that snow to a rope-bridge over a ravine with a river at the bottom. You may have seen such. They prodded him behind like an ox. 'Damn your eyes!' says the King. 'D'you suppose I can't die like a gentleman?' He turns to Peachey—Peachey that was crying like a child. 'I've brought you to this, Peachey,' says he. 'Brought you out of your happy life to be killed in Kafiristan, where you was late Commander-in-Chief of the Emperor's forces. Say you forgive me, Peachey.' 'I do,' says Peachey. 'Fully and freely do I forgive you, Dan.' 'Shake hands, Peachey,' says he. 'I'm going now.' Out he goes, looking neither right nor left, and when he was plumb in the middle of those dizzy dancing ropes, 'Cut, you beggars,' he shouts; and they cut, and old Dan fell, turning round and round and round twenty thousand miles, for he took half an hour to fall till he struck the water, and I could see his body caught on a rock with the gold crown close beside.

"But do you know what they did to Peachey between two pine trees? They crucified him, Sir, as Peachey's hand will show. They used wooden pegs for his hands and his feet; and he didn't die. He hung there and screamed, and they took him down next day, and said it was a miracle he wasn't dead. They took him down—poor old Peachey that hadn't done them any harm—that hadn't done them any . . ."

He rocked to and fro and wept bitterly, wiping his eyes

with the back of his scarred hands and moaning like a child for some ten minutes.

"They was cruel enough to feed him up in the temple, because they said he was more of a God than old Daniel that was a man. Then they turned him out on the snow, and told him to go home, and Peachey came home in about a year, begging alone the roads quite safe; for Daniel Dravot he walked before and said:—'Come along, Peachey. It's a big thing we're doing.' The mountains they danced at night, and the mountains they tried to fall on Peachey's head, but Dan he held up his hand, and Peachey came along bent double. He never let go of Dan's hand, and he never let go of Dan's head. They gave it to him as a present in the temple, to remind him not to come again, and though the crown was pure gold, and Peachey was starving, never would Peachey sell the same. You knew Dravot, Sir! You knew Right Worshipful Brother Dravot! Look at him now!"

He fumbled in the mass of rags round his bent waist; brought out a black horsehair bag embroidered with silver thread; and shook therefrom on to my table—the dried, withered head of Daniel Dravot! The morning sun that had long been paling the lamps struck the red beard and blind sunken eyes; struck, too, a heavy circlet of gold studded with raw turquoises, that Carnehan had placed tenderly on the battered temples.

"You behold now!" said Carnehan, "the Emperor in his habit as he lived—the King of Kafiristan with his crown upon his head. Poor old Daniel that was a monarch once!"

I shuddered, for, in spite of defacements manifold, I

recognized the head of the man of Marwar Junction. Carnehan rose to go. I attempted to stop him. He was not fit to walk abroad. "Let me take away the whiskey, and give me a little money," he gasped. "I was a King once. I'll go to the Deputy Commissioner and ask to set in the Poorhouse till I get my health. No, thank you, I can't wait till you get a carriage for me. I've urgent private affairs—in the south—at Marwar."

He shambled out of the office and departed in the direction of the Deputy Commissioner's house. That day at noon I had occasion to go down the blinding hot Mall, and I saw a crooked man crawling along the white dust of the roadside, his hat in his hand, quavering dolorously after the fashion of street-singers at Home. There was not a soul in sight, and he was out of all possible earshot of the houses. And he sang through his nose, turning his head from right to left:

> "The Son of Man goes forth to war,
>   A golden crown to gain;
> His blood-red banner streams afar—
>   Who follows in his train?"

I waited to hear no more, put the poor wretch into my carriage and drove him off to the nearest missionary for eventual transfer to the Asylum. He repeated the hymn twice while he was with me whom he did not in the least recognize, and I left him singing it to the missionary.

Two days later I inquired after his welfare of the Superintendent of the Asylum.

"He was admitted suffering from sunstroke. He died early yesterday morning," said the Superintendent. "Is it true that he was half an hour bareheaded in the sun at midday?"

"Yes," said I, "but do you happen to know if he had anything upon him by any chance when he died?"

"Not to my knowledge," said the Superintendent.

And there the matter rests.

WITHOUT BENEFIT OF CLERGY

I

"But if it be a girl?"

"Lord of my life, it cannot be! I have prayed for so many nights, and sent gifts to Sheikh Badl's shrine so often, that I know God will give us a son—a man-child that shall grow into a man. Think of this and be glad. My mother shall be his mother till I can take him again, and the mullah of the Pattan Mosque shall cast his nativity—God send he be born in an auspicious hour!—and then, and then thou wilt never weary of me, thy slave."

"Since when hast thou been a slave, my queen?"

"Since the beginning—till this mercy came to me. How could I be sure of thy love when I knew that I had been bought with silver?"

"Nay, that was the dowry. I paid it to thy mother."

"And she has buried it, and sits upon it all day long like a hen. What talk is yours of dowry? I was bought as though I had been a Lucknow dancing-girl instead of a child."

"Art thou sorry for the sale?"

"I have sorrowed; but to-day I am glad. Thou wilt never cease to love me now? Answer, my king."

"Never—never. No."

"Not even though the *mem-log*—the white women of thy own blood—love thee? And remember, I have watched them driving in the evening; they are very fair."

"I have seen fire-balloons by the hundred, I have seen the moon, and—then I saw no more fire-balloons."

63

Ameera clapped her hands and laughed. "Very good talk," she said. Then, with an assumption of great stateliness: "It is enough. Thou hast my permission to depart—if thou wilt."

The man did not move. He was sitting on a low red-lacquered couch in a room furnished only with a blue-and-white floor-cloth, some rugs, and a very complete collection of native cushions. At his feet sat a woman of sixteen, and she was all but all the world in his eyes. By every rule and law she should have been otherwise, for he was an Englishman and she a Mussulman's daughter, bought two years before from her mother, who, being left without money, would have sold Ameera, shrieking, to the Prince of Darkness, if the price had been sufficient.

It was a contract entered into with a light heart. But even before the girl had reached her bloom she came to fill the greater portion of John Holden's life. For her and the withered hag her mother he had taken a little house overlooking the great red-walled city, and found, when the marigolds had sprung up by the well in the courtyard, and Ameera had established herself according to her own ideas of comfort, and her mother had ceased grumbling at the inadequacy of the cooking-places, the distance from the daily market, and matters of housekeeping in general, that the house was to him his home. Any one could enter his bachelor's bungalow by day or night, and the life that he led there was an unlovely one. In the house in the city his feet only could pass beyond the outer court-yard to the women's rooms; and when the big wooden gate was bolted behind him he was king in his own territory, with Ameera for queen. And there was going to be added to this kingdom a third person, whose arrival Holden felt inclined to resent. It interfered with his perfect happiness. It disarranged the orderly peace of the house that was his own. But Ameera was wild with delight at the thought of it, and her mother not less so. The love of a man, and particularly a white man, was at the best an inconstant affair, but it might, both women argued, be held fast by a baby's hands. "And then," Ameera would always say— "then he will never care for the white *mem-log*. I hate them all—I hate them all!"

"He will go back to his own people in time," said the mother, "but, by the blessing of God, that time is yet afar off."

Holden sat silent on the couch, thinking of the future, and his thoughts were not pleasant. The drawbacks of a double life are manifold. The government, with singular care, had ordered him out of the station for a fortnight on special duty, in the place of a man who was watching by the bedside of a sick wife. The verbal notification of the transfer had been edged by a cheerful remark that Holden ought to think himself lucky in being a bachelor and a free man. He came to break the news to Ameera.

"It is not good," she said slowly, "but it is not all bad. There is my mother here, and no harm will come to me—unless, indeed, I die of pure joy. Go thou to thy work, and think no troublesome thoughts. When the days are done, I believe . . . nay, I am sure. And—and then I shall lay *him* in thy arms, and thou wilt love me forever. The train goes to-night—at midnight, is it not? Go now, and do not let thy heart be heavy by cause of me. But thou will not delay in returning! Thou wilt not stay on the road to talk to the bold white *mem-log*! Come back to me swiftly, my life!"

As he left the court-yard to reach his horse, that was teth-ered to the gate-post, Holden spoke to the white-haired old watchman who guarded the house, and bid him under certain contingencies dispatch the filled-up telegraph form that Holden gave him. It was all that could be done, and, with the sensations of a man who has attended his own funeral, Holden went away by the night mail to his exile. Every hour of the day he dreaded the arrival of the telegram, and every hour of the night he pictured to himself the death of Ameera. In consequence, his work for the state was not of first-rate quality, nor was his temper toward his colleagues of the most amiable. The fortnight ended without a sign from his home, and, torn to pieces by his anxieties, Holden returned to be swallowed up for two precious hours by a dinner at the club, where he heard, as a man hears in a swoon, voices telling him how execrably he had performed the other man's duties, and how he had endeared himself to all his associates. Then he fled on horseback through the night with his heart in his mouth. There was no answer at first to his blows on the gate, and he had just wheeled his horse round to kick it in, when Pir Khan appeared with a lantern and held his stirrup.

"Has aught occurred?" said Holden.

"The news does not come from my mouth, Protector of the Poor, but"— He held out his shaking hand, as befitted the bearer of good news who is entitled to a reward.

Holden hurried through the court-yard. A light burned in the upper room. His horse neighed in the gateway, and he heard a pin-pointed wail that sent all the blood into the apple of his throat. It was a new voice, but it did not prove that Ameera was alive.

"Who is there?" he called up the narrow brick staircase.

There was a cry of delight from Ameera, and then the voice of her mother, tremulous with old age and pride: "We be two women, and—the—man—thy son."

On the threshold of the room Holden stepped on a naked dagger that was laid there to avert ill-luck, and it broke at the hilt under his impatient heel.

"God is great!" cooed Ameera in the half-light. "Thou hast taken his misfortunes on thy head."

"Ay, but how is it with thee, life of my life? Old woman, how is it with her?"

"She has forgotten her sufferings for joy that the child is born. There is no harm; but speak softly," said the mother.

"It only needed thy presence to make me all well," said Ameera. "My king, thou hast been very long away. What gifts hast thou for me? Ah, ah! It is I that bring gifts this time. Look, my life, look! Was there ever such a babe? Nay, I am too weak even to clear my arm from him."

"Rest, then, and do not talk. I am here, *bachheri*" (little woman).

"Well said, for there is a bond and a heel-rope (*peecharee*) between us now that nothing can break. Look —canst thou see in this light? He is without spot or blemish. Never was such a man-child. *Ya illah!* he shall be a pundit—no, a trooper of the queen. And, my life, dost thou love me as well as ever, though I am faint and sick and worn? Answer truly."

"Yea. I love as I have loved, with all my soul. Lie still, pearl, and rest."

"Then do not go. Sit by my side here—so. Mother, the lord of this house needs a cushion. Bring it." There was an almost imperceptible movement on the part of the new life that lay in the hollow of Ameera's arm. "Aho!" she said, her voice breaking with love. "The babe is a champion from his birth. He is kicking me in the side with mighty kicks. Was there ever such a babe? And he is ours to us—thine and mine. Put thy hand on his head, but carefully, for he is very young, and men are unskilled in such matters."

Very cautiously Holden touched with the tips of his fingers the downy head.

"He is of the Faith," said Ameera; "for, lying here in the night-watches, I whispered the Call to Prayer and the Profession of Faith into his ears. And it is most marvelous that he was born upon a Friday, as I was born. Be careful of him, my life; but he can almost grip with his hands."

Holden found one helpless little hand that closed feebly on his finger. And the clutch ran through his limbs till it settled about his heart. Till then his sole thought had been for Ameera. He began to realize that there was some one else in the world, but he could not feel that it was a veritable son with a soul. He sat down to think, and Ameera dozed lightly.

"Get hence, sahib," said her mother, under her breath.

"It is not good that she should find you here on waking. She must be still."

"I go," said Holden, submissively. "Here be rupees. See that my *baba* gets fat and finds all that he needs."

The chink of the silver roused Ameera. "I am his mother, and no hireling," she said, weakly. "Shall I look to him more or less for the sake of money? Mother, give it back. I have borne my lord a son."

The deep sleep of weakness came upon her almost before the sentence was completed. Holden went down to the court-yard very softly, with his heart at ease. Pir Khan, the old watchman, was chuckling with delight.

"This house is now complete," he said, and without further comment thrust into Holden's hands the hilt of a sabre worn many years ago, when Pir Khan served the queen in the police. The bleat of a tethered goat came from the well-curb.

"There be two," said Pir Khan—"two goats of the best. I bought them, and they cost much money; and since there is no birth-party assembled, their flesh will be all mine. Strike craftily, sahib. 'Tis an ill-balanced sabre at the best. Wait till they raise their heads from cropping the marigolds."

"And why?" said Holden, bewildered.

"For the birth sacrifice. What else? Otherwise the child, being unguarded from fate, may die. The Protector of the Poor knows the fitting words to be said."

Holden had learned them once, with little thought that he would ever say them in earnest. The touch of the cold sabre-hilt in his palm turned suddenly to the clinging grip

of the child upstairs—the child that was his own son—
and a dread of loss filled him.

"Strike!" said Pir Khan. "Never life came into the
world but life was paid for it. See, the goats have raised
their heads. Now! With a drawing cut!"

Hardly knowing what he did, Holden cut twice as he
muttered the Mohammedan prayer that runs: "Almighty!
In place of this my son I offer life for life, blood for blood,
head for head, bone for bone, hair for hair, skin for skin."
The waiting horse snorted and bounded in his pickets at
the smell of the raw blood that spurted over Holden's rid-
ing-boots.

"Well smitten!" said Pir Khan, wiping the sabre "A
swordsman was lost in thee. Go with a light heart, heaven
born. I am thy servant and the servant of thy son. May
the Presence live a thousand years, and . . . the flesh of the
goats is all mine?"

Pir Khan drew back richer by a month's pay. Holden
swung himself into the saddle and rode off through the low-
hanging wood smoke of the evening. He was full of
riotous exultation, alternating with a vast vague tender-
ness directed toward no particular object, that made him
choke as he bent over the neck of his uneasy horse. "I
never felt like this in my life," he thought. "I'll go to
the club and pull myself together."

A game of pool was beginning, and the room was full
of men. Holden entered, eager to get to the light and the
company of his fellows, singing at the top of his voice:

"'In Baltimore a-walking, a lady I did meet.'"

"Did you?" said the club secretary from his corner.

"Did she happen to tell you that your boots were wringing wet? Great goodness, man, it's blood!"

"Bosh!" said Holden, picking his cue from the rack. "May I cut in? It's dew. I've been riding through high crops. My faith! my boots are a mess, though!

> " 'And if it be a girl, she shall wear a wedding ring;
> And if it be a boy, he shall fight for his king;
> With his dirk and his cap, and his little jacket blue,
> He shall walk the quarter-deck' "—

"Yellow and blue—green next player," said the marker, monotonously.

" 'He shall walk the quarter-deck'—am I green, marker? —'he shall walk the quarter-deck'—ouch! that's a bad shot!—'as his daddy used to do!' "

"I don't see that you have anything to crow about," said a zealous junior civilian, acidly. "The government is not exactly pleased with your work when you relieved Sanders."

"Does that mean a wigging from headquarters?" said Holden, with an abstracted smile. "I think I can stand it."

The talk beat up round the ever-fresh subject of each man's work, and steadied Holden till it was time to go to his dark, empty bungalow, where his butler received him as one who knew all his affairs. Holden remained awake for the greater part of the night, and his dreams were pleasant ones.

II

"How old is he now?"

"*Ya illah!* What a man's question! He is all but six

weeks old; and on this night I go up to the house-top with thee, my life, to count the stars. For that is auspicious. And he was born on a Friday, under the sign of the Sun, and it has been told to me that he will outlive us both and get wealth. Can we wish for aught better, beloved?"

"There is nothing better. Let us go up to the roof, and thou shalt count the stars—but a few only, for the sky is heavy with cloud."

"The winter rains are late, and maybe they come out of season. Come, before all the stars are hid. I have put on my richest jewels."

"Thou hast forgotten the best of all."

"Ai! *Ours.* He comes also. He has never yet seen the skies."

Ameera climbed the narrow staircase that led to the flat roof. The child, placid and unwinking, lay in the hollow of her right arm, gorgeous in silver-fringed muslin, with a small skull-cap on his head. Ameera wore all that she valued most. The diamond nose-stud that takes the place of the Western patch in drawing attention to the curve of the nostril, the gold ornament in the centre of the forehead studded with tallow-drop emeralds and flawed rubies, the heavy circlet of beaten gold that was fastened round her neck by the softness of the pure metal, and the chinking curb-patterned silver anklets hanging low over the rosy ankle-bone. She was dressed in jade-green muslin, as befitted a daughter of the Faith, and from shoulder to elbow and elbow to wrist ran bracelets of silver tied with floss silk, frail glass bangles slipped over the wrist in proof of the slenderness of the hand, and certain heavy gold bracelets that had no part in her country's ornaments, but since they were Holden's gift, and fastened with a cunning European snap, delighted her immensely.

They sat down by the low white parapet of the roof, overlooking the city and its lights.

"They are happy down there," said Ameera. "But I do not think that they are as happy as we. Nor do I think the white *mem-log* are as happy. And thou?"

"I know they are not."

"How dost thou know?"

"They give their children over to the nurses."

"I have never seen that," said Ameera, with a sigh, "nor do I wish to see. Ahi!"—she dropped her head on Holden's shoulder—"I have counted forty stars, and I am tired. Look at the child, love of my life. He is counting, too."

The baby was staring with round eyes at the dark of the heavens. Ameera placed him in Holden's arms, and he lay there without a cry.

"What shall we call him among ourselves?" she said "Look! Art thou ever tired of looking? He carries thy very eyes! But the mouth—"

"Is thine, most dear. Who should know better than I?"

" 'Tis such a feeble mouth. Oh, so small! And yet it holds my heart between its lips. Give him to me now. He has been too long away."

"Nay, let him lie; he has not yet begun to cry."

"When he cries thou wilt give him back, eh? What a man of mankind thou art! If he cried, he were only the dearer to me. But, my life, what little name shall we give him?"

The small body lay close to Holden's heart. It was utterly helpless and very soft. He scarcely dared to breathe for fear of crushing it. The caged green parrot, that is regarded as a sort of guardian spirit in most native households, moved on its perch and fluttered a drowsy wing.

"There is the answer," said Holden. "Mian Mittu has spoken. He shall be the parrot. When he is ready he will talk mightily, and run about. Mian Mittu is the parrot in thy—in the Mussulman tongue, is it not?"

"Why put me so far off?" said Ameera, fretfully. "Let it be like unto some English name—but not wholly. For he is mine."

"Then call him Tota, for that is likest English."

"Ay, Tota; and that is still the parrot. Forgive me, my lord, for a minute ago; but, in truth, he is too little to wear all the weight of Mian Mittu for name. He shall be Tota —our Tota to us. Hearest thou, oh, small one? Littlest, thou art Tota."

She touched the child's cheek, and he, waking, wailed, and it was necessary to return him to his mother, who soothed him with the wonderful rhyme of "*Aré koko, Ja ré koko!*" which says:

"Oh, crow! Go crow! Baby's sleeping sound,
And the wild plums grow in the jungle, only a penny a pound—
Only a penny a pound, *Baba*—only a penny a pound."

Reassured many times as to the price of those plums, Tota cuddled himself down to sleep. The two sleek white well-bullocks in the court-yard were steadily chewing the cud of their evening meal; old Pir Khan squatted at the head of Holden's horse, his police sabre across his knees, pulling drowsily at a big water-pipe that croaked like a bull-frog in a pond. Ameera's mother sat spinning in the lower veranda, and the wooden gate was shut and barred. The music of a marriage procession came to the roof above the gentle hum of the city, and a string of flying-foxes crossed the face of the low moon.

"I have prayed," said Ameera, after a long pause, with her chin in her hand—"I have prayed for two things. First, that I may die in thy stead, if thy death is demanded; and in the second, that I may die in the place of the child. I have prayed to the Prophet and to Beebee Miriam.[1] Thinkest thou either will hear?"

"From thy lips who would not hear the lightest word?"

"I asked for straight talk, and thou hast given me sweet talk. Will my prayers be heard?"

"How can I say? God is very good."

"Of that I am not sure. Listen now. When I die or the child dies, what is thy fate? Living, thou wilt return to the bold white *mem-log*, for kind calls to kind."

"Not always."

"With a woman, no. With a man it is otherwise. Thou wilt in this life, later on, go back to thine own folk. That I could almost endure, for I should be dead. But in thy very death thou wilt be taken away to a strange place and a paradise that I do not know."

"Will it be paradise?"

"Surely; for what God would harm thee? But we two—I and the child—shall be elsewere, and we cannot come to thee, nor canst thou come to us. In the old days, before the child was born, I did not think of these things; but now I think of them perpetually. It is very hard talk."

[1] The Virgin Mary

"It will fall as it will fall. To-morrow we do not know, but to-day and love we know well. Surely we are happy now."

"So happy that it were well to make our happiness assured. And thy Beebee Miriam should listen to me; for she is also a woman. But then she would envy me— It is not seemly for men to worship a woman."

Holden laughed aloud at Ameera's little spasm of jealousy.

"It is not seemly? Why didst thou not turn me from worship of thee, then?"

"Thou a worshipper! And of me! My king, for all thy sweet words, well I know that I am thy servant and thy slave, and the dust under thy feet. And I would not have it otherwise. See!"

Before Holden could prevent her she stooped forward and touched his feet; recovering herself with a little laugh, she hugged Tota closer to her bosom. Then, almost savagely:

"Is it true that the bold white *mem-log* live for three times the length of my life? Is it true that they make their marriages not before they are old women?"

"They marry as do others—when they are women."

"That I know, but they wed when they are twenty-five. Is that true?"

"That is true."

"*Ya illah!* At twenty-five! Who would of his own will take a wife even of eighteen? She is a woman—aging every hour. Twenty-five! I shall be an old woman at that age, and— Those *mem-log* remain young forever. How I hate them!"

"What have they to do with us?"

"I cannot tell. I know only that there may now be alive on this earth a woman ten years older than I who may come to thee and take thy love ten years after I am an old woman, grey-headed, and the nurse of Tota's son. That is unjust and evil. They should die too."

"Now, for all thy years thou art a child, and shalt be picked up and carried down the stair-case."

"Tota! Have a care for Tota, my lord! Thou, at least, art as foolish as any babe!" Ameera tucked Tota out of harm's way in the hollow in her neck, and was carried downstairs, laughing, in Holden's arms, while Tota opened his eyes and smiled, after the manner of the lesser angels.

He was a silent infant, and almost before Holden could realize that he was in the world, developed into a small gold-colored godling and unquestioned despot of the house overlooking the city. Those were months of absolute happiness to Holden and Ameera—happiness withdrawn from the world, shut in behind the wooden gate that Pir Khan guarded. By day Holden did his work, with an immense pity for such as were not so fortunate as himself, and a sympathy for small children that amazed and amused many mothers at the little station gatherings. At nightfall he returned to Ameera—Ameera full of the wondrous doings of Tota; how he had been seen to clap his hands together and move his fingers with intention and purpose, which was manifestly a miracle; how, later, he had of his own initiative crawled out of his low bedstead on to the floor, and swayed on both feet for the space of three breaths.

"And they were long breaths, for my heart stood still with delight," said Ameera.

Then he took the beasts into his councils—the well-bullocks, the little grey squirrels, the mongoose that lived in a hole near the well, and especially Mian Mittu, the parrot, whose tail he grievously pulled, and Mian Mittu screamed till Ameera and Holden arrived.

"Oh, villain! Child of strength! This is to thy brother on the house-top! *Tobah, tobah!* Fy! fy! But I know a charm to make him wise as Suleiman and Aflatoun.[1] Now look," said Ameera. She drew from an embroidered bag a handful of almonds. "See! we count seven. In the name of God!" She placed Mian Mittu, very angry and rumpled, on the top of his cage, and, seating herself between the babe and the bird, cracked and peeled an almond less white than her teeth. "This is a true charm, my life; and do not laugh. See! I give the parrot one half and Tota the other." Mian Mittu, with careful beak, took his share from beneath Ameera's lips, and she kissed the other half into the mouth of the child, who eat it slowly, with wondering eyes. "This I will do each day of seven, and without doubt he who is ours will be a bold speaker and wise. Eh, Tota, what wilt thou be when thou art a man and I am grey-headed?" Tota tucked his fat legs into adorable creases. He could crawl, but he was not going to waste the spring of his youth in idle speech. He wanted Mian Mittu's tail to tweak.

When he was advanced to the dignity of a silver belt —which, with a magic square engraved on silver and hung

1 Solomon and Plato

round his neck, made up the greater part of his clothing—
he staggered on a perilous journey down the garden to Pir
Khan, and proffered him all his jewels in exchange for one
little ride on Holden's horse. He had seen his mother's
mother chaffering with peddlers in the veranda. Pir Khan
wept, set the untried feet on his own grey head in sign
of fealty, and brought the bold adventurer to his mother's
arms, vowing that Tota would be a leader of men ere
his beard was grown.

One hot evening, while he sat on the roof between his
father and mother, watching the never-ending warfare of
the kites that the city boys flew, he demanded a kite of
his own, with Pir Khan to fly it, because he had a fear of
dealing with anything larger than himself; and when Holden
called him a "spark," he rose to his feet and answered
slowly, in defense of his new-found individuality: *"Hum
'park nahin hai. Hum admi hai."* (I am no spark, but
a man.)

The protest made Holden choke, and devote himself
very seriously to a consideration of Tota's future.

He need hardly have taken the trouble. The delight of
that life was too perfect to endure. Therefore it was taken
away, as many things are taken away in India, suddenly
and without warning. The little lord of the house, as Pir
Khan called him, grew sorrowful and complained of pains,
who had never known the meaning of pain. Ameera,
wild with terror, watched him through the night, and in
the dawning of the second day the life was shaken out of
him by fever—the seasonal autumn fever. It seemed al-
together impossible that he could die, and neither Ameera
nor Holden at first believed the evidence of the body on

the bedstead. Then Ameera beat her head against the
wall, and would have flung herself down the well in the
garden had Holden not restrained her by main force.

One mercy only was granted to Holden. He rode to
his office in broad daylight, and found waiting him an
unusually heavy mail that demanded concentrated attention and hard work. He was not, however, alive to this
kindness of the gods.

III

The first shock of the bullet is no more than a brisk
pinch. The wrecked body does not send in its protest to
the soul till ten or fifteen seconds later. Then comes
thirst, throbbing, and agony, and a ridiculous amount of
screaming. Holden realized his pain slowly, exactly as
he had realized his happiness, and with the same imperious
necessity for hiding all trace of it. In the beginning he
only felt that there had been a loss, and that Ameera needed
comforting where she sat with her head on her knees, shivering as Mian Mittu, from the house-top, called "Tota!
Tota! Tota!" Later all his world and the daily life of it
rose up to hurt him. It was an outrage that any one of
the children at the band-stand in the evening should be
alive and clamorous when his own child lay dead. It was
more than mere pain when one of them touched him, and
stories told by overfond fathers of their children's latest
performances cut him to the quick. He could not declare
his pain. He had neither help, comfort, nor sympathy, and
Ameera, at the end of each weary day, would lead him
through the hell of self-questioning reproach which is re-

served for those who have lost a child, and believe that with a little—just a little—more care it might have been saved. There are not many hells worse than this, but he knows one who has sat down temporarily to consider whether he is or is not responsible for the death of his wife.

"Perhaps," Ameera would say, "I did not take sufficient heed. Did I, or did I not? The sun on the roof that day when he played so long alone, and I was—*ahi!* braiding my hair—it may be that the sun then bred the fever. If I had warned him from the sun he might have lived. But, oh, my life, say that I am guiltless! Thou knowest that I loved him as I loved thee! Say that there is no blame on me, or I shall die—I shall die!"

"There is no blame. Before God, none. It was written, and how could we do aught to save? What has been, has been. Let it go, beloved."

"He was all my heart to me. How can I let the thought go when my arm tells me every night that he is not here? *Ahi! ahi!* Oh, Tota, come back to me—come back again, and let us be all together as it was before!"

"Peace! peace! For thine own sake, and for mine also, if thou lovest me, rest."

"By this I know thou dost not care; and how shouldst thou? The white men have hearts of stone and souls of iron. Oh, that I had married a man of mine own people —though he beat me—and had never eaten the bread of an alien!"

"Am I an alien, mother of my son?"

"What else, sahib? . . . Oh, forgive me—forgive! The death has driven me mad. Thou art the life of my heart, and the light of my eyes, and the breath of my life, and —and I have put thee from me, though it was but for a moment. If thou goest away, to whom shall I look for help? Do not be angry. Indeed, it was the pain that spoke, and not thy slave."

"I know—I know. We be two who were three. The greater need, therefore, that we should be one."

They were sitting on the roof, as of custom. The night was a warm one in early spring, and sheet-lightning was dancing on the horizon to a broken tune played by far-off thunder. Ameera settled herself in Holden's arms.

"The dry earth is lowing like a cow for the rain, and I —I am afraid. It was not like this when we counted the stars. But thou lovest me as much as before, though a bond is taken away? Answer."

"I love more, because a new bond has come out of the sorrow that we have eaten together; and that thou knowest."

"Yea, I know," said Ameera, in a very small whisper. "But it is good to hear thee say so, my life, who art so strong to help. I will be a child no more, but a woman and an aid to thee. Listen. Give me my *sitar*, and I will sing bravely."

She took the light silver-studded *sitar*, and began a song of the great hero Rajá Rasalu. The hand failed on the strings, the tune halted, checked, and at a low note turned off to the poor little nursery rhyme about the wicked crow:

" 'And the wild plums grow in the jungle, only a penny a pound—
    Only a penny a pound, *Baba*—only' "—

Then came the tears and the piteous rebellion against fate, till she slept, moaning a little in her sleep, with the right arm thrown clear of the body, as though it protected something that was not there.

It was after this night that life became a little easier for Holden. The ever-present pain of loss drove him into his work, and the work repaid him by filling up his mind for eight or nine hours a day. Ameera sat alone in the house and brooded, but grew happier when she understood that Holden was more at ease, according to the custom of women. They touched happiness again, but this time with caution.

"It was because we loved Tota that he died. The jealousy of God was upon us," said Ameera. "I have hung up a large black jar before our window to turn the Evil Eye from us, and we must make no protestations of delight, but go softly underneath the stars, lest God find us out. Is that not good talk, worthless one?"

She had shifted the accent of the word that means "beloved," in proof of the sincerity of her purpose. But the kiss that followed the new christening was a thing that any deity might have envied. They went about henceforth saying: "It is naught—it is naught," and hoping that all the powers heard.

The powers were busy on other things. They had allowed thirty million people four years of plenty, wherein men fed well and the crops were certain and the birthrate rose year by year; the districts reported a purely agricultural population varying from nine hundred to two thousand to the square mile of the over-burdened earth. It was time to make room. And the Member for Lower Tooting, wandering about India in top-hat and frock-coat, talked largely of the benefits of British rule, and suggested

as the one thing needful the establishment of a duly qual-
ified electoral system and a general bestowal of the fran-
chise. His long-suffering hosts smiled and made him wel-
come, and when he paused to admire, with pretty picked
words, the blossom of the blood-red dhak-tree, that had
flowered untimely for a sign of the sickness that was coming, they smiled more than ever.

It was the Deputy Commissioner of Kot-Kumharsen,
staying at the club for a day, who lightly told a tale
that made Holden's blood run cold as he overheard the
end.

"He won't bother any one any more. Never saw a
man so astonished in my life. By Jove! I thought he
meant to ask a question in the House about it. Fellow-
passenger in his ship—dined next him—bowled over by
cholera, and died in eighteen hours. You needn't laugh,
you fellows. The Member for Lower Tooting is awfully
angry about it; but he's more scared. I think he's going
to take his enlightened self out of India."

"I'd give a good deal if he were knocked over. It might
keep a few vestrymen of his kidney to their parish. But
what's this about cholera? It's full early for anything of
that kind," said a warden of an unprofitable salt-lick.

"Dunno," said the deputy commissioner, reflectively.
"We've got locusts with us. There's sporadic cholera all
along the north—at least, we're calling it sporadic for
decency's sake. The spring crops are short in five districts, and nobody seems to know where the winter rains
are. It's nearly March now. I don't want to scare any-
body, but it seems to me that Nature's going to audit her
accounts with a big red pencil this summer."

"Just when I wanted to take leave, too," said a voice across the room.

"There won't be much leave this year, but there ought to be a great deal of promotion. I've come in to persuade the government to put my pet canal on the list of famine-relief works. It's an ill wind that blows no good. I shall get that canal finished at last."

"Is it the old programme, then," said Holden—"famine, fever, and cholera?"

"Oh, no! Only local scarcity and an unusual prevalence of seasonal sickness. You'll find it all in the reports if you live till next year. You're a lucky chap. You haven't got a wife to put you out of harm's way. The hill-stations ought to be full of women this year."

"I think you're inclined to exaggerate the talk in the bazaars," said a young civilian in the secretariat. "Now, I have observed—"

"I dare say you have," said the deputy commissioner, "but you've got a great deal more to observe, my son. In the meantime, I wish to observe to you"— And he drew him aside to discuss the construction of the canal that was so dear to his heart.

Holden went to his bungalow, and began to understand that he was not alone in the world, and also that he was afraid for the sake of another, which is the most soul-satisfying fear known to man.

Two months later, as the deputy had foretold, Nature began to audit her accounts with a red pencil. On the heels of the spring reapings came a cry for bread, and the government, which had decreed that no man should die of want, sent wheat. Then came the cholera from all four quarters of the compass. It struck a pilgrim gathering of half a million at a sacred shrine. Many died at the feet of their god, the others broke and ran over the face of the land, carrying the pestilence with them. It smote a walled city and killed two hundred a day. The people crowded the trains, hanging on to the footboards and squatting on the roofs of the carriages; and the cholera followed them, for at each station they dragged out the dead and the dying on the platforms reeking of lime-wash and carbolic acid. They died by the roadside, and the horses of the Englishmen shied at the corpses in the grass. The rains did not come, and the earth turned to iron lest man should escape by hiding in her. The English sent their wives away to the Hills, and went about their work, coming forward as they were bidden to fill the gaps in the fighting line. Holden, sick with fear of losing his chiefest treasure on earth, had done his best to persuade Ameera to go away with her mother to the Himalayas.

"Why should I go?" said she one evening on the roof.

"There is sickness, and the people are dying, and all the white *mem-log* have gone."

"All of them?"

"All—unless, perhaps, there remain some old scald-head who vexes her husband's heart by running risk of death."

"Nay; who stays is my sister, and thou must not abuse her, for I will be a scald-head too. I am glad all the bold white *mem-log* are gone."

"Do I speak to a woman or a babe? Go to the Hills, and I will see to it that thou goest like a queen's daughter. Think, child! In a red-lacquered bullock-cart, veiled and

curtained, with brass peacocks upon the pole and red-cloth
hangings. I will send two orderlies for guard, and"—

"Peace! Thou art the babe in speaking thus. What
use are those toys to me? *He* would have patted the bul-
locks and played with the housings. For his sake, perhaps
—thou hast made me very English—I might have gone.
Now I will not. Let the *mem-log* run."

"Their husbands are sending them, beloved."

"Very good talk. Since when hast thou been my husband to tell me what to do? I have but borne thee a son.
Thou art only all the desire of my soul to me. How shall
I depart when I know that if evil befall thee by the breadth
of so much as my littlest finger-nail—is that not small?
—I should be aware of it though I were in Paradise? And
here, this summer thou mayest die—ai, Janee, die!—and
in dying they might call to tend thee a white woman, and
she would rob me in the last of thy love."

"But love is not born in a moment, or on a deathbed."

"What dost thou know of love, stone-heart? She would
take thy thanks at least, and, by God and the Prophet and
Beebee Miriam, the mother of thy Prophet, that I will
never endure. My lord and my love, let there be no
more foolish talk of going away. Where thou art, I am.
It is enough." She put an arm round his neck and a hand
on his mouth.

There are not many happinesses so complete as those
that are snatched under the shadow of the sword. They
sat together and laughed, calling each other openly by
every pet name that could move the wrath of the gods.
The city below them was locked up in its own torments.
Sulphur-fires blazed in the streets; the conches in the

Hindoo temples screamed and bellowed, for the gods were inattentive in those days. There was a service in the great Mohammedan shrine, and the call to prayer from the minarets was almost unceasing. They heard the wailing in the houses of the dead, and once the shriek of a mother who had lost a child and was calling for its return. In the grey dawn they saw the dead borne out through the city gates, each litter with his own little knot of mourners. Wherefore they kissed each other and shivered.

It was a red and heavy audit, for the land was very sick and needed a little breathing-space ere the torrent of cheap life should flood it anew. The children of immature fathers and undeveloped mothers made no resistance. They were cowed and sat still, waiting till the sword should be sheathed in November, if it were so willed. There were gaps among the English, but the gaps were filled. The work of superintending famine relief, cholera-sheds, medicine distribution, and what little sanitation was possible, went forward because it was so ordered.

Holden had been told to hold himself in readiness to move to replace the next man who should fall. There were twelve hours in each day when he could not see Ameera, and she might die in three. He was considering what his pain would be if he could not see her for three months, or if she died out of his sight. He was absolutely certain that her death would be demanded—so certain that, when he looked up from the telegram and saw Pir Khan breathless in the doorway, he laughed aloud, "And?" —said he.

"When there is a cry in the night and the spirit flutters into the throat, who has a charm that will restore? Come swiftly, heaven born. It is the black cholera."

Holden galloped to his home. The sky was heavy with clouds, for the long-deferred rains were at hand, and the heat was stifling. Ameera's mother met him in the court-yard, whimpering: "She is dying. She is nursing herself into death. She is all but dead. What shall I do, sahib?"

Ameera was lying in the room in which Tota had been born. She made no sign when Holden entered, because the human soul is a very lonely thing, and when it is get-ting ready to go away hides itself in a misty border-land where the living may not follow. The black cholera does its work quietly and without explanation. Ameera was being thrust out of life as though the Angel of Death had himself put his hand upon her. The quick breathing seemed to show that she was either afraid or in pain, but neither eyes nor mouth gave any answer to Holden's kisses. There was nothing to be said or done. Holden could only wait and suffer. The first drops of the rain began to fall on the roof, and he could hear shouts of joy in the parched city.

The soul came back a little and the lips moved. Holden bent down to listen. "Keep nothing of mine," said Ameera. "Take no hair from my head. *She* would make thee burn it later on. That flame I should feel. Lower! Stoop lower! Remember only that I was thine and bore thee a son. Though thou wed a white woman to-morrow, the pleasure of taking in thy arms thy first son is taken from thee forever. Remember me when thy son is born—the one that shall carry thy name before all men. His mis-fortunes be on my head. I bear witness—I bear witness"

—the lips were forming the words on his ear—"that there is no God but—thee, beloved."

Then she died. Holden sat still, and thought of any kind was taken from him till he heard Ameera's mother lift the curtain.

"Is she dead, sahib?"

"She is dead."

"Then I will mourn, and afterward take an inventory of the furniture in this house; for that will be mine. The sahib does not mean to resume it. It is so little, so very little, sahib, and I am an old woman. I would like to lie softly."

"For the mercy of God, be silent awhile! Go out and mourn where I cannot hear."

"Sahib, she will be buried in four hours."

"I know the custom. I shall go ere she is taken away. That matter is in thy hands. Look to it that the bed—on which—on which—she lies"—

"Aha! That beautiful red-lacquered bed. I have long desired"—

—"That the bed is left here untouched for my disposal. All else in the house is thine. Hire a cart, take everything, go hence, and before sunrise let there be nothing in this house but that which I have ordered thee to respect."

"I am an old woman. I would stay at least for the days of mourning, and the rains have just broken. Whither shall I go?"

"What is that to me? My order is that there is a going. The house-gear is worth a thousand rupees, and my orderly shall bring thee a hundred rupees to-night."

"That is very little. Think of the cart-hire."

"It shall be nothing unless thou goest, and with speed. Oh, woman, get hence, and leave me to my dead!"

The mother shuffled down the staircase, and in her anxiety to take stock of the house-fittings forgot to mourn. Holden stayed by Ameera's side, and the rain roared on the roof. He could not think connectedly by reason of the noise, though he made many attempts to do so. Then four sheeted ghosts glided dripping into the room and stared at him through their veils. They were the washers of the dead. Holden left the room and went out to his horse. He had come in a dead, stifling calm, through ankle-deep dust. He found the court-yard a rain-lashed pond alive with frogs, a torrent of yellow water ran under the gate, and a roaring wind drove the bolts of the rain like buckshot against the mud walls. Pir Khan was shivering in his little hut by the gate, and the horse was stamping uneasily in the water.

"I have been told the sahib's order," said he. "It is well. This house is now desolate. I go also, for my monkey face would be a reminder of that which has been. Concerning the bed, I will bring that to thy house yonder in the morning. But remember, sahib, it will be to thee as a knife turned in a green wound. I go upon a pilgrimage and I will take no money. I have grown fat in the protection of the Presence, whose sorrow is my sorrow. For the last time I hold his stirrup."

He touched Holden's foot with both hands, and the horse sprang out into the road, where the creaking bamboos were whipping the sky and all the frogs were chuckling. Holden could not see for the rain in his face. He put his hands before his eyes and muttered: "Oh, you brute! You utter brute!"

The news of his trouble was already in his bungalow. He read the knowledge in his butler's eyes when Ahmed Khan brought in food, and for the first and last time in his life laid a hand upon his master's shoulder, saying: "Eat, sahib, eat. Meat is good against sorrow. I also have known. Moreover, the shadows come and go, sahib. The shadows come and go. These be curried eggs."

Holden could neither eat nor sleep. The heavens sent down eight inches of rain in that night and scoured the earth clean. The waters tore down walls, broke roads, and washed open the shallow graves in the Mohammedan burying-ground. All next day it rained, and Holden sat still in his house considering his sorrow. On the morning of the third day he received a telegram which said only: "Ricketts, Myndonie. Dying. Holden. Relieve. Immediate." Then he thought that before he departed he would look at the house wherein he had been master and lord. There was a break in the weather. The rank earth steamed with vapor, and Holden was vermilion from head to heel with the prickly-heat born of sultry moisture.

He found that the rains had torn down the mud-pillars of the gateway, and the heavy wooden gate that had guarded his life hung drunkenly from one hinge. There was grass three inches high in the court-yard; Pir Khan's lodge was empty, and the sodden thatch sagged between the beams. A grey squirrel was in possession of the veranda, as if the house had been untenanted for thirty years instead of three days. Ameera's mother had removed everything except some mildewed matting. The *tick-tick* of the little scorpions as they hurried across the floor was the only sound in the house. Ameera's room and that other one where Tota had lived were heavy with mildew, and the narrow staircase leading to the roof was streaked and stained with rain-borne mud. Holden saw all these things, and came out again to meet in the road Durga Dass, his landlord—portly, affable, clothed in white muslin, and driving a C-spring buggy. He was over-looking his property, to see how the roofs withstood the stress of the first rains.

"I have heard," said he, "you will not take this place any more, sahib?"

"What are you going to do with it?"

"Perhaps I shall let it again."

"Then I will keep it on while I am away."

Durga Dass was silent for some time. "You shall not take it on, sahib," he said. "When I was a young man I also— But to-day I am a member of the municipality. Ho! Ho! No. When the birds have gone, what need to keep the nest? I will have it pulled down; the timber will sell for something always. It shall be pulled down, and the municipality shall make a road across, as they desire, from the burning-ghat to the city wall. So that no man may say where this house stood."

INTERNATIONAL : POCKET : LIBRARY

1. MADEMOISELLE FIFI   *Guy de Maupassant*
   Introduction by Joseph Conrad

2. TWO TALES   *Rudyard Kipling*
   Foreword by Wilson Follett

3. TWO WESSEX TALES   *Thomas Hardy*
   Introduction by Conrad Aiken

4. MODERN RUSSIAN CLASSICS
   Stories by Andreyev, Solgub, Gorki, Tchekov,
   Babel, and Artzibashev. Foreword by Issac Goldberg

5. CANDIDE   *Voltaire*
   Introduction by Andre Morize

6. THE LAST LION   *Vicente Blasco Ibáñez*
   Introduction by Mariano Joaquin Lorente

7. A SHROPSHIRE LAD   *A. E. Housman*
   Preface by William Stanley Braithwaite

8. GITANJALI   *Rabindranath Tagore*
   Introduction by W. B. Yeats

9. THE BOOK OF FRANÇOIS VILLON
   Introduction by H. De Vere Stacpoole

10. THE HOUND OF HEAVEN   *Francis Thompson*
    Introduction by G. K. Chesterton

11. COLOURED STARS   Edited by *Edward Powys Mathers*

12. RUBAIYAT OF OMAR KHAYYAM   *Edward Fitzgerald*
    With Decorations by Elihu Vedder

OTHER TITLES IN PREPARATION

INTERNATIONAL : POCKET : LIBRARY

13. THE IMPORTANCE OF BEING EARNEST *Oscar Wilde*

14. FIVE MODERN PLAYS *O'Neill, Schnitzler, Dunsany, Maeterlinck, Richard Hughes*

15. THREE IRISH PLAYS *J. M. Synge, Douglas Hyde, and W. B. Yeats*
    Introduction by Harrison Hale Schaff

16. THE GREATEST THING IN THE WORLD
    Henry Drummond
    Introduction by Elizabeth Towne

17. THE SYMPOSIUM OF PLATO
    Introduction by *B. Jowett, M.A.*

18. THE WISDOM OF CONFUCIUS
    Edited by *Miles M. Dawson*

19. ALICE IN WONDERLAND *Lewis Carroll*
    Illustrated by Sir John Tenniel

20. THROUGH THE LOOKING-GLASS *Lewis Carroll*
    Illustrated by Sir John Tenniel

OTHER TITLES IN PREPARATION